The kiss deepened without any help on his part.

He wanted more. And he couldn't have stopped himself from taking it.

And then she was gone. Ripped away.

She bolted from the rocker, her chest rising and falling as she backed up against the split-pine railing surrounding the porch. "I'm sorry. I shouldn't have done that."

"But you did."

"I got caught up. That can't happen again."

Her expression glittered with undisguised longing. So why was she stopping?

"I heartily disagree. It's practically a requirement for it to happen again."

"Are you that clueless, Kyle? I'm your daughters' caseworker," she reminded him with raised eyebrows. "We can't get involved."

His body cooled faster than if she'd dumped a bucket of ice water on his head. "You're right."

Of course she was right. This wasn't about whether she was interested or not; it was about his daughters. What had started out as a half-formed plan to distract her from work had actually distracted *him* far more effectively.

And he wanted to do it again.

* * *

The SEAL's Secret H
Th
Lies and
schem

Dear Reader,

I've long been a huge fan of the Texas Cattlemen's Club series, and I'm thrilled to be bringing you one more story from Royal! By now you've met some of the new faces and know that the town has been rebuilt after the devastating tornado...but that's not the end of the drama in store for our residents.

Kyle Wade is home in Royal, the last place he wants to be. He never planned to come back after Grace Haines broke his heart, but here he is—co-owner of a ranch he's determined to help manage and father of twin girls he didn't know existed. The only thing standing in the way of starting this new phase of his life is none other than Grace...and she's never forgiven *or* forgotten Kyle.

I loved telling this story of a former SEAL turned cowboy and father. Kyle has so many hurdles to overcome, but he's a "get things done" kind of guy, and his journey to find a place where he belongs is both heart-wrenching and sweet. Thanks for coming along with me on this ride!

Don't miss Liam's story, Kyle's twin brother, in *Nanny Makes Three* by Cat Schield.

Readers are the reason I write books. Connect with me at katcantrell.com.

Kat

THE SEAL'S SECRET HEIRS

KAT CANTRELL

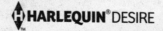

Special thanks and acknowledgment are given to Kat Cantrell for her contribution to the Texas Cattleman's Club: Lies and Lullabies series.

ISBN-13: 978-0-373-73445-0

The SEAL's Secret Heirs

Recycling programs for this product may not exist in your area.

Printed in U.S.A.

www.Harlequin.com

Kat Cantrell read her first Harlequin novel in third grade and has been scribbling in notebooks since she learned to spell. What else would she write but romance?

Kat, her husband and their two boys live in north Texas. When she's not writing about characters on the journey to happily-ever-after, she can be found at a soccer game, watching the TV show *Friends* or listening to '80s music.

Kat was the 2011 Harlequin So You Think You Can Write contest winner and a 2012 RWA Golden Heart® Award finalist for best unpublished series contemporary manuscript.

Books by Kat Cantrell

Harlequin Desire

Marriage with Benefits
The Things She Says
The Baby Deal
Pregnant by Morning
The Princess and the Player
Triplets Under the Tree

Happily Ever After, Inc.

Matched to a Billionaire
Matched to a Prince
Matched to Her Rival

Newlywed Games

From Ex to Eternity
From Fake to Forever

Texas Cattleman's Club: Lies and Lullabies

The SEAL's Secret Heirs

Visit her Author Profile page at Harlequin.com, or katcantrell.com, for more titles!

To Cat Schield. Thanks for all the collaboration and for being my guide into the TCC world!

One

Royal, Texas was the perfect place to go to die.

Kyle Wade aimed to do exactly that. After an honorable discharge from the navy, what else lay ahead of him but a slow and painful death? Might as well do it in Royal, the town that had welcomed every Wade since the dawn of time—except him.

He nearly drove through the center of town without stopping. Because he hadn't realized he was *in* Royal until he was nearly *out* of Royal.

Yeah, it had been ten years, and when he'd stopped for gas in Odessa, he'd heard about the tornado that had ripped through the town. But still. Was nothing on the main strip still the same? These new buildings hadn't been there when he'd left. Of course, he'd hightailed it out of Royal for Coronado, California, in a hurry and hadn't looked back once in all his years as a Navy SEAL. Had he really expected Royal to be suspended in time, like a photograph?

He kind of had.

Kyle slowed as he passed the spot where he'd first kissed Grace Haines in the parking lot of the Dairy Queen. Or what used to be the spot where he'd taken his high school girlfriend on their first date. The Dairy Queen had moved down the road and in its place stood a little pink building housing something called Mimi's Nail Salon. Really?

Fitting that his relationship with Grace had nothing to mark it. Nothing in Royal proper anyway. The scars on his heart would always be there.

Shaking his head, Kyle punched the gas. He had plenty of time to gawk at the town later and no time to think about the woman who had driven him into the military. His shattered leg hurt something fierce and he'd been traveling for the better part of three days. It was time to go home.

And now he had a feeling things had probably changed at Wade Ranch—also known as home—more than he'd have anticipated. Never the optimist, he suspected that meant they'd gotten worse. Which was saying something, since he'd left in the first place because of the rift with his twin brother, Liam. No time like the present to get the cold welcome over with.

Wade Ranch's land unrolled at exactly the ten-mile marker from Royal. At least *that* was still the same. Acres and acres of rocky, hilly countryside spread as far as Kyle could see. Huh. Reminded him of Afghanistan. Wouldn't have thought there'd be any comparison, but there you go. A man could travel ten thousand miles and still wind up where he started. In more ways than one.

The gate wasn't barred. His brother, Liam, was running a loose ship apparently. Their grandfather had died a while back and left the ranch to both brothers, but Kyle had never intended to claim his share. Yeah, it was a significant inheritance. But he didn't want it. He wanted his team back and his life as a SEAL. An insurgent's spray of bullets had guaranteed that would never happen. Even if

Kyle hadn't gotten shot, Cortez was gone and no amount of wishing or screaming at God could bring his friend and comrade-in-arms back to life.

Hadn't stopped Kyle from trying.

Kyle drove up the winding lane to the main house, which had a new coat of paint. The white Victorian house had been lording over Wade land for a hundred years, but looked like Liam had done some renovation. The tire swing that had hung from the giant oak in the front yard was gone and a new porch rocker with room for two had been added.

Perfect. Kyle could sit there in that rocker and complain about how the coming rain was paining his joints. Maybe later he could get up a game of dominos at the VA with all of the other retired military men. *Retired.* They might as well call it dead.

When Kyle jumped from the cab of the truck he'd bought in California after the navy decided they were done with him, he hit the dusty ground at the wrong angle. Pain shot up his leg and it stole his breath for a moment. When a man couldn't even get out of his own truck without harm, it was not a good day.

Yeah, he should be more careful. But then he'd have to admit something was wrong with this leg.

He sucked it up. *The only easy day was yesterday.* That mantra had gotten him through four tours of duty in the Middle East. Surely it could get him to the door of Wade Ranch.

It did. Barely. He knocked, but someone was already answering before the sound faded.

The moment the door swung open, Kyle stepped over the threshold and did a double take. *Liam.* His brother stood in the middle of the renovated foyer, glowering. He'd grown up and out in ten years. Kyle had, too, of course, but it was still a shock to see that his brother had changed from the picture he'd carried in his mind's eye, even though their faces mostly matched.

Crack!

Agony exploded across Kyle's jaw as his head snapped backward.

What in the… Had Liam just *punched* him?

Every nerve in Kyle's body went on full alert, vibrating with tension as he reoriented and automatically began scanning both the threat of Liam and the perimeter simultaneously. The foyer was empty, save the two Wade brothers. And Liam wasn't getting the drop on him twice.

"That's for not calling," Liam said succinctly and balled his fists as if he planned to go back for seconds.

"Nice to see you, too."

Dang. Talking hurt. Kyle spit out a curse along with a trickle of blood that hit the hardwood floor an inch from Liam's broken-in boot.

"Deadbeat. You have a lot of nerve showing up now. Get gone or there's more where that came from."

Liam clearly had no idea who he was tangling with.

"I don't cater much to sucker punches," Kyle drawled, and touched his lower lip, right above where the throb in his jaw hurt the worst. Blood came away with his finger. "Why don't you try that again now that I'm paying attention?"

Liam shook his head wearily, his fists going slack. "Your face is as hard as your head. Why now? After all this time, why did you finally drag your sorry butt home?"

"Aww. Careful there, brother, or people might start thinking you missed me something fierce when you talk like that."

Liam had another thirty seconds to explain why Kyle's welcome home had included a fist. Liam had a crappy right hook, but it still hurt. If anything, Kyle was the one who should be throwing punches. After all, he was the one with the ax to grind. He was the one who had left Royal because of what Liam had done.

Or rather *whom* he'd done. Grace Haines. Liam had broken the most sacred of all brotherly bonds when he messed around with the woman Kyle loved. Afghanistan wasn't far enough away to forget, but it was the farthest a newly minted SEAL could go after being deployed.

So he hadn't forgotten. Or forgiven.

"I called your cell phone," Liam said. "I called every navy outpost I could for two months straight. I left messages. I called about the messages. Figured that silence was enough of an answer." Arms crossed, Liam looked down his nose at Kyle, which was a feat, given that they were the same height. "So I took steps to work through this mess you've left in my lap."

Wait, he'd gotten punched over leaving the ranch in his brother's capable hands? That was precious. Liam had loved Wade Ranch from the first, maybe even as early as the day their mother had dropped them off with Grandpa and never came back.

"You were always destined to run Wade Ranch," Kyle said, and almost didn't choke on it. "I didn't dump it on you."

Liam snorted. "Are you really that dense? I'm not talking about the ranch, moron. I'm talking about your kids."

Kyle flinched involuntarily. "My...what?"

Kids? As in children?

"Yes, kids," Liam enunciated, drawing out the *i* sound as if Kyle might catch his meaning better if the word had eighteen syllables. "Daughters. Twins. I don't get why you waited to come home. You should have been here the moment you found out."

"I'm finding out *this* moment," Kyle muttered as his pulse kicked up, beating in his throat like a May hailstorm on a tin roof. "How...wha..."

His throat closed.

Twin daughters. And Liam thought they were *his*? Someone had made a huge mistake. Kyle didn't have any children. Kyle didn't *want* any children.

Liam was staring at him strangely. "You didn't get my messages?"

"Geez, Liam. What was your first clue? I wasn't sitting at a desk dodging your calls. I spent six months in…a bad place and then ended up in a worse place."

From the city of Kunduz to Landstuhl Regional, the US-run military hospital in Germany. He didn't remember a lot of it, but the incredible pain as the doctors worked to restore the bone a bullet had shattered in his leg—that he would never forget.

But he was one of the lucky ones who'd survived his wounds. Cortez hadn't. Kyle still had nightmares about leaving his teammate behind in that foxhole where they'd been trapped by insurgents. Seemed wrong. Cortez should have had a proper send-off for his sacrifice.

"Still not a chatterbox, I see." Liam scrubbed at his face with one hand, and when he dropped it, weariness had replaced the glower. "Keep your secrets about your fabulous life overseas as a badass. I really don't care. I have more important things to get straight."

The weariness was new. Kyle remembered his brother as being a lot of things—a betrayer, first and foremost—but not tired. It looked wrong on his face. As wrong as the constant pain etched into Kyle's own face when he looked in the mirror. Which was why he'd quit looking in the mirror.

"Why don't you start at the beginning." Kyle jerked his head toward what he hoped was still the kitchen. "Maybe we can hash it out over tea?"

It was too early in the morning for Jack Daniel's, though he might make an exception, pending the outcome of the conversation.

Liam nodded and spun to stride off toward the back of the house. Following him, Kyle was immediately blinded by all the off-white cabinets in the kitchen. His brother hadn't left a stone unturned when he'd gotten busy redoing the house. Modern appliances in stainless steel had replaced the old harvest gold ones and new double islands dominated the center. A wall of glass overlooked the back acreage that stretched for miles until it hit Old Man Drucker's property. Or what had been Drucker's property ten years ago. Obviously Kyle wasn't up-to-date about what had been going on since he'd left.

Without ceremony, Liam splashed some tea into a cup from a pitcher on the counter and shoved the cup into his hand. "Tea. Now talk to me about Margaret Garner."

Hot. Blonde. Nice legs. Kyle visualized the woman instantly. But that was a name he hadn't thought about in—wow, like almost a year.

"Margaret Garner? What does she have to do with any—"

The question died in his throat. *Almost a year.* Like long enough to grow a baby or two? Didn't mean it was true. Didn't mean they were his babies.

It felt like a really good time to sit down, and he thought maybe he could do it without tipping off Liam how badly his leg ached 24-7.

He fell heavily onto a bar stool at the closest island, tea forgotten and shoulders ten pounds heavier. "San Antonio. She was with a group of friends at Cantina Juarez. A place where military groupies hang out."

"So you did sleep with her?"

"Not that it's any of your business," Kyle said noncommittally. They were long past the kiss-and-tell stage of their relationship, if they'd ever been that close. When Liam took up with Grace ten years ago, it had killed any fragment of warmth between them, warmth that was unlikely to return.

"You made it my business when you didn't come home to take care of your daughters," Liam countered, as his fists balled up again.

"Take another swing at me and you'll get real cozy with the floor in short order." Kyle contemplated his brother. Who was furious. "So Margaret came around with some babies looking for handouts? I hope you asked for a paternity test before you wrote a check."

This was bizarre. Of all the conversations he'd thought he'd be having with Liam, this was not it. *Babies. Margaret. Paternity test.* None of these things made sense, together or separately.

Why hadn't any of Liam's messages been relayed? Probably because he hadn't called the right office—by design. Kyle hadn't exactly made it clear how Liam could reach him. Maybe it was a blessing that Kyle hadn't known. He couldn't have hopped on a plane anyway.

Kyle couldn't be a father. He barely knew how to be a civilian and had worked long and hard at accepting that he wasn't part of a SEAL team any longer.

It was twice as hard to accept that after being discharged, he had nowhere to go but back to the ranch where he'd never fit in, never belonged. His injury wasn't supposed to be a factor as he figured out what to do with the rest of his life, since God hadn't seen fit to let him die alongside Cortez. But being a father—to twins, no less—meant he had to think about what a busted leg meant for a man's everyday life. And he did not like thinking about how difficult it was some days to simply stand.

Liam threw up a hand, a scowl crawling onto his expression. "Shut up a minute. No one wrote any checks. You're the father of the babies, no question."

Well, Kyle had a few questions. Like why Margaret hadn't contacted him when she found out she was pregnant. While Liam had little information on his whereabouts,

Margaret sure knew how to get in touch. Her girlfriend had been dating Cortez and called him all the time. She'd known exactly where he was stationed.

It was nothing short of unforgivable. "Where's Margaret?"

"She died," Liam bit out shortly. "While giving birth. It's a long story. Do I need to give you a minute?"

Kyle processed that much more slowly than he would have liked. Margaret was dead? It seemed like just yesterday that he'd spent a long weekend with her in a hotel room. She'd been a wildcat, determined to send him back to Afghanistan with enough memories to keep him warm at night, as she'd put it.

He was sad to learn Margaret had passed, sure. He'd liked thinking about her on the other side of the world, living a normal life that he was helping to secure by going after bad guys. But they'd spent less than forty-eight hours together and had barely known each other, by design. He wasn't devastated—it wasn't as if he'd lost the love of his life or anything. Not like when he'd lost Grace.

"We used protection," he muttered. As if that was the most important thing to get straight at this point. "I don't understand. How did she get pregnant?"

"The normal way, I imagine. Moron." Liam rolled his eyes the way he'd always done when they were younger. "Do you have any interest whatsoever in meeting your daughters?"

Kyle blinked. "Well…yeah. Of course. What happened to them after Margaret died? Who's taking care of them?"

"I am. Me and Hadley. Who's the most amazing woman. She's the nanny I hired when you didn't respond to any of my calls."

Reeling, Kyle tried to gather some of his wits, but they seemed as scattered and filmy as clouds on a mild spring day. "Thanks. That's… You didn't have to. That's above the call of duty."

Liam crossed his arms, biceps rippling under the sleeve of his T-shirt. "They're great babies. Beautiful. And I didn't do it for you. I did it because I love them. Hadley and I, we're planning to keep on taking care of them, too."

"That's not going to happen. You've spent the last ten minutes whaling on me about not coming home to take responsibility for this. I'm here. I'm man enough to step up." He set his jaw, which still throbbed. "I want to see them."

The atmosphere fairly vibrated with animosity as they stared each other down, neither blinking, neither backing down. Something flickered through Liam's gaze and he gave one curt nod.

"Fine." Liam called up the stairs off the kitchen that led to the upper stories.

After the longest three minutes of Kyle's life, he heard footsteps and a pretty, blonde woman who must be the nanny came down the stairs. But Kyle only had eyes for the pink bundles, one each in the crook of her arms.

Sucker punch number two.

Those were real, live, honest-to-God babies. What the hell was he thinking, saying that he wanted to see them? What was that supposed to prove? That he didn't know squat about babies?

They were so small. Nearly identical. Twins, like Kyle and Liam. He'd always heard that identical twins skipped generations, but apparently not.

"What are their names?" he whispered.

"Madeline and Margaret Wade," the woman responded, and the babies lifted their heads toward the sound of her voice. Clearly she'd spent a lot of time with them. "We call them Maddie and Maggie for short."

Somehow that seemed perfect for their little wrinkled faces. "Can I hold them?"

"Sure. This is Maggie." She handed over the first one and cheerfully helped Kyle get the baby situated without being asked, which he appreciated more than he could possibly say because his stupid hands suddenly seemed too clumsy to handle something so breakable.

Hey, little girl. He couldn't talk over the lump in his throat, and no one seemed inclined to make him, so he just looked at her. His heart thumped as it expanded, growing larger the longer he held his daughter. That was a kick in the pants. Who would have thought you could instantly love someone like that? It should have taken time. But there it was.

Now what? What if she cried? What if *he* cried?

He'd hoped a flood of knowledge would magically appear if he could just get his hands on the challenge. You didn't learn to hack through vegetation with a machete until you put it in your palm and started hacking.

"You can take her back," he said gruffly, overwhelmed with all the emotion he had no idea what to do with. But there was still another one. Another daughter. He found new appreciation for the term *double trouble.*

"This one is Maddie," the woman said.

Somehow, the other pink bundle ended up in his arms. Instantly, he could tell she was smaller, weighing less than her sister. Strange. She felt even more fragile than her sister, as if Kyle should be careful how heavily he breathed or he might blow her to the ground with an extra big huff.

Equal parts love and fierce devotion surged through the heart he'd already thought was full, splitting it open. She'd need someone to look out for her. To protect her.

That's on me. My job.

And then being a father made all the sense in the world. These were his girls. The reason he wasn't dead in a foxhole flopped out next to Cortez right now. The Almighty got it perfectly right some days.

"And this is Hadley Wade, my wife," Liam broke in with

the scowl that seemed to be a permanent part of his face nowadays. "We still introduce ourselves in these parts."

"It's okay," Hadley said with a hand on Liam's elbow. Her palm settled into the crook comfortably, as if they were intimate often. "Give him a break. It's a lot to take in."

"I'm done." Kyle rubbed his free hand across his military-issue buzz cut, but it didn't stimulate his brain much. He contemplated Hadley, the woman Liam had casually mentioned that he'd married, as if that was some small thing. "I don't think there's much more I can take in. I appreciate what you've done in my stead, but these are my girls. I want to be their father, in all the ways that count. I'm here and I'm sticking around Royal."

That hadn't been set in his mind until this moment. But it would take a bulldozer to shove him onto a different path now.

"Well, it's not as simple as all that," Liam corrected. "Their mama is gone and you weren't around. So even though I have temporary custody, these girls became wards of the state and had a social worker assigned. You're gonna have to deal with the red tape before you start joining the PTA and picking out matching Easter dresses."

Wearily, Kyle nodded. "I get that. What do I have to do?"

Hadley and Liam exchanged glances and a sense of foreboding rose up in Kyle's stomach.

With a sigh, Liam pulled out his cell phone. "I'll call their social worker. But before she gets here, you should know that it's Grace Haines."

Grace. The name hit him in the solar plexus and all the air rushed from his lungs.

Sucker punch number three.

Grace Haines had avoided looking at the date all day, but it sneaked up on her after lunch. She stared at the letters and numbers she'd just typed on a case file.

March 12. The third anniversary of the day she'd become a Professional Single Girl. She should get cake. Or a card. Something to mark the occasion of when she'd given up the ghost and decided to be happy with her career as a social worker. Instead of continually dating men who were nice enough, but could never live up to her standards, she'd learn to be by herself.

Was it so wrong to want a man who doted on her as her father did with her mother? She wasn't asking for much. Flowers occasionally. A text message here and there with a heart emoticon and a simple thinking of you. Something that showed Grace was a priority. That the guy noticed when she wasn't there.

Yeah, that was dang difficult, apparently. The decision to stop actively looking for Mr. Right and start going to museums and plays as a party of one hadn't been all that hard. As a bonus, she never had to compromise on date night by seeing a science fiction movie where special effects drowned out the dialogue. She could do whatever she wanted with her Saturday nights.

It was great. Or at least that was what she told herself. Loudly. It drowned out the voice in her heart that kept insisting she would never get the family she desperately wanted if she didn't date.

In lieu of a Happy Professional Single Girl cake, Grace settled for a Reese's Peanut Butter Cup from the vending machine and got back to work. The children's cases the county had entrusted to her were not going to handle themselves, and there were some heartbreakers in her caseload. She loved her job and thanked God every day she got to make a difference in the lives of the children she helped.

If she couldn't have children of her own, she'd make do with loving other people's.

Her desk phone rang and she picked up the receiver, accidentally knocking over the framed picture of her mom and dad celebrating their thirtieth wedding anniversary at a luau in Hawaii. One day she'd go there, she vowed as she righted the frame. Even if she had to travel to Hawaii solo, it was still Hawaii.

"Grace Haines. How can I help you today?"

"It's Liam," the voice on the other end announced, and the gravity in his tone tripped her radar.

"Are the girls all right?" Panicked, Grace threw a couple of manila folders into her tote in preparation to fly to her car. She could be at Wade Ranch in less than twenty minutes if she ignored the speed limit and prayed to Jesus that Sheriff Battle wasn't sitting in his squad car at the Royal city limits the way he usually did. "What's happened to the babies? It's Maddie, isn't it? I knew that she wasn't—"

"The girls are fine," he interrupted. "They're with Hadley. It's Kyle. He came home."

Grace froze, mid-file transfer. The manila folder fell to the floor in slow motion from her nerveless fingers, opened at the spine and spilled papers across the linoleum.

"What?" she whispered.

Kyle.

Her first kiss. Her first love. Her first taste of the agonizing pain a man could cause.

He wasn't supposed to be here. The twin daughters Kyle Wade had fathered were parentless, or so she'd convinced herself. That was the only reason she'd taken the case, once Liam assured her he'd called the USO, the California base Kyle had shipped out of and the President of the United States. No response, he'd said.

No response meant no conflict of interest.

If Kyle was back, her interest was so conflicted, she couldn't even see through it.

"He's here. At Wade Ranch," Liam confirmed. "You need to come by as soon as possible and help us sort this out."

Translation: Liam and Hadley wanted to adopt Maddie and Maggie and with Kyle in the picture, that wasn't as easy as they'd all assumed. Grace would have to convince him to waive his parental rights. If he didn't want to, then she'd have to assess Kyle's fitness as a parent and potentially even give him custody, despite knowing in her heart that he'd be a horrible father. It was a huge tangle.

The best scenario would be to transfer the case to someone else. But on short notice? Probably wasn't going to happen.

"I'll be there as soon as I can. Thanks, Liam. It'll work out."

Grace hung up and dropped her head down into the crook of her elbow.

Somehow, she was supposed to go to Wade Ranch and do her job, while ignoring the fact that Kyle Wade had broken her heart into tiny little pieces, and then promptly joined the military, as if she hadn't mattered at all. And somehow, she had to ignore the fact that she still wasn't over it. Or him.

Two

Grace knocked on the door of Wade House and steeled herself for whatever was about to happen. Which was what she'd been doing in the car on the way over. And at her desk before that.

No one else in the county office could take on another case, so Grace had agreed to keep Maddie and Maggie under the premise that she'd run all her recommendations through her supervisor before she told the parties involved about her decisions. Which meant she couldn't just decide ahead of time that Kyle wasn't fit. She had to prove it.

It would be a stringent process, with no room for error. She'd have to justify her report with far more data and impartial observations than she'd ever had to before. It meant twice as many visits and twice as much documentation. Of course. Because who didn't want to spend a bunch of time with a high-school boyfriend who'd ruined you for dating any other man?

Hopefully, he'd just give up his rights without a fight and they could all go on.

The door swung open and Grace forgot to breathe. Kyle Wade was indeed home.

Hungrily, her gaze skittered over his grown-up face. *Oh, my.* Still gorgeous, but sun worn, with new lines around his eyes that said he'd seen some things in the past ten years and they weren't all pleasant. His hair was shorn shorter than short, but it fit this new version of Kyle.

His green eyes were diamond hard. That was new, too. He'd never been open and friendly, but she'd burrowed under that reserve back in high school and when he really looked at her with his signature blend of love and devotion—it had been magic.

She instantly wanted to burrow under that hardness once again. Because she knew she was the only one who could, the only one he'd let in. The only one who could soothe his loneliness, the way she'd done back then.

Gah, what was she *thinking*?

She couldn't focus on that. Couldn't remember what it had been like when it was good, because when it was bad, it was really bad. This man had destroyed her, nearly derailing her entire first year at college as she picked up the broken pieces he'd left behind.

"Hey, Grace."

Kyle's voice washed over her and the steeling she'd done to prepare for this moment? Useless.

"Kyle," she returned a bit brusquely, but if she started blubbering, she'd never forgive herself. "I'm happy to see that you've finally decided to acknowledge your children."

Chances were good that wouldn't last. He'd ship out again at a moment's notice, running off to indulge his selfish thirst for adventure, leaving behind a mess. As he'd done the first time. But Grace was here to make sure he didn't hurt anyone in the process, least of all those precious babies.

"Yep," he agreed easily. "I took a slow boat from China all right. But I'm here now. Do whatever you have to do to make it okay with the county for me to be a father to my daughters."

Ha. Fathers were loving, caring, selfless. They didn't become distant and uncommunicative on a regular basis and then forget they had plans with you. And then forget to apologize for leaving you high and dry. Nor did they have the option to quit when the going got tough.

"Well, that's not going to happen today," she said firmly. "I'll do several site visits to make sure that you're providing the right environment for the girls. They need to feel safe and loved and it's my job to put them into the home that will give them that. You might not be the best answer."

The hardness in his expression intensified. "They're mine. I'll take care of them."

His quiet fierceness set her back. Guess that answered the question about whether he'd put up a token fight and then sign whatever she put in front of him that would terminate his parental rights. The fact that he wasn't—it was throwing her for a loop. "Actually, they're mine. They became wards of the state when you didn't respond to the attempts we all made to find you. That's what happens to abandoned babies."

That might have come out harshly. So what. It was the truth, even if the sentiment had some leftover emotion from when Kyle had done that to her. She had to protect the babies, no matter what.

"There were…circumstances. I didn't get any of Liam's messages or I would have come as soon as I could." His mouth firmed into an inflexible line. "That's not important now. Come in and visit. Tell me what I have to do."

"Fine."

She followed him into the formal parlor that had been restored to what she imagined was Wade House's former glory. The Victorian furniture was beautiful and luxurious, and a man like Kyle looked ridiculous sitting on the elegantly appointed chair. Good grief, the spindly legs didn't seem strong enough to support such a solid body. Kyle had gained weight, and the way he moved indicated it was 100 percent finely honed muscle under his clothes. He'd adopted a lazy, slow walk that seemed at odds with all that, but certainly fit a laid-back cowboy at home on his ranch.

Not that she'd noticed or anything.

She took her own seat and perched on the edge, too keyed up to relax. "We'll need to fill out some paperwork. What do you plan to do for employment now that you're home?"

Kyle quirked an eyebrow. "Being a Wade isn't enough?"

Frowning, she held her manila folder in front of her like a shield, though what she thought it was going to protect her from, she had no idea. Kyle's diamond-bit green eyes drilled through her very flesh and bone, deep into the soft places she'd thought were well protected against men. Especially this one.

"No, it's not enough. Inheriting money isn't an indicator of your worth as a parent. I need to see a demonstration of commitment. A permanency that will show you can provide a stable environment for Maddie and Maggie."

"So being able to buy them whatever they want and being able to put food on the table no matter what isn't good enough."

It was not a question but a challenge. She tried not to roll her eyes, she really did. But if you looked up "clueless" in the dictionary, you'd see a picture of Kyle Wade. "That's right. Liam and Hadley can do those things and have been for over two months. Are you prepared for all the special treatments and doctor's visits Maddie will require? I have to know."

Kyle went stiff all at once, freezing so quickly that she got a little concerned. She should really stop caring so much but it was impossible to shut off her desire to help people. This whole conversation was difficult. She and Kyle used to be comfortable with each other. She missed that easiness between them, but there was no room for anything other than a professional and necessary distance.

"Doctor's visits?" Kyle repeated softly. "Is there something wrong with Maddie?"

"Maddie suffers from twin-to-twin transfusion syndrome. She has some heart problems that are pretty serious."

"I...didn't know."

The bleakness in his expression reached out and twisted her heart. She wanted to lash out at him. Blame him. Those girls had been fighting for their lives after Margaret died, and where was Kyle? "Just out of curiosity, why did you come home now? Why not two months ago when Margaret first came looking for you? Or for that matter, why not when she first found out she was pregnant?"

She cut off the tirade there. Oh, there was plenty more she wanted to say, but it would veer into personal barbs that wouldn't help anything. She had a job to do and the information-gathering stage should—and would—stay on a professional level.

Besides, she knew he'd been stationed overseas. He probably hadn't had the luxury of jetting off whenever he felt like it. But he could have at least called.

Crossing his arms, he leaned back against the gold velvet cushions of the too-small chair, biceps bulging. He'd grown some interesting additions to what had already been a nicely built body. Automatically, her gaze wandered south, taking in all the parts that made up that great physique. Wow, had it gotten hot in here, or what? She fanned her face with the manila folder.

But then he eyed her, his face a careful mask that dared her to break through it. Which totally unnerved her. This darker, harder, fiercer Kyle Wade was dangerous. Because she wanted to understand why he was dark, hard and fierce. Why he'd broken her heart and then left.

"You got me all figured out, seems like," he drawled. "Why don't you tell me why I didn't hop on a plane and stick by Margaret's side during her pregnancy?"

Couldn't the man just answer a simple question? He'd always been like this—uncommunicative and prone to leaving instead of dealing with problems head-on. His attitude was so infuriating, she said the first thing that popped into her head.

"Guilt, probably. You didn't want to be involved and hoped the problem would go away on its own." And that was totally unfair. Wasn't it? She had no idea why he hadn't contacted anyone. This new version of Kyle was unsettling *because* she didn't know him that well anymore.

Really, she wasn't that good at reading people in the first place. It was a professional weakness that she hated, but couldn't seem to fix. Once upon a time, she'd thought this man was her forever after, her Prince Charming, Clark Gable and Dr. McDreamy all rolled into one. Which was totally false. She'd bought heavily into that lie, so how could she trust her own judgment? She couldn't. That's why she had to be so methodical in her approach to casework, because she couldn't afford to let emotion rule her decisions. Or afford to make a mistake, not when the future of a child was at stake.

And she wouldn't do either here. Maddie and Maggie deserved a loving home with a family who paid attention to their every need. Kyle Wade was not the right man for that, no matter what he said he wanted.

"Well, then," he said easily. "Guess that answers your question."

It so did not. She still didn't know why he'd come home now, why he'd suddenly shown an interest in his daughters. Whether he could possibly convince her he planned to stick around—if he was even serious about that. Kyle had a habit of running away from his problems, after all.

First and foremost, how could she assess whether the time-hardened man before her could ever provide the loving, nurturing environment two fragile little girls needed?

But she'd let it slide for now. There was plenty of time to work through all of that, since Maddie and Maggie were still legally in the care of Liam and Hadley.

"I think I have enough for now. I'll file my first report and send you a copy when it's approved." She had to get out of here. Before she broke down under the emotional onslaught of everything.

"That's it, huh? What's the report going to say?"

"It's going to say that you've expressed an interest in retaining your parental rights and that I've advised you that I can't approve that until I do several more site visits."

He cocked his head, evaluating her coolly. "How long is that going to take?"

"Until I'm satisfied with your fitness as a parent. Or until I decide you're unfit. At which point I'll make recommendations as to what I believe is the best home for those precious girls. I will likely recommend they stay with Liam and Hadley."

Without warning, Kyle was on his feet, an intense vibe rippling down his powerful body. She'd have sworn he hadn't moved, and then all of a sudden, there he was, staring down at her with a sharpness about him, as if he'd homed in on her and her alone. She couldn't move, couldn't breathe.

It was precisely the kind of focus she'd craved once. But not now. Not like this.

"Why would you give my kids to my brother?" he asked, his voice dangerously low.

"Well, the most obvious reason is because he and Hadley want them. They've already looked into adoption. But also because they know the babies' needs and have already been providing the best place for the girls."

"You are not taking away my daughters," he said succinctly. "Why does this feel personal?"

She blinked. "This is the opposite of personal, Kyle. My job is to be the picture of impartiality. Our history has nothing to do with this."

"I was starting to wonder if you recalled that we had a history," he drawled slowly, loading the words with meaning.

The intensity rolling from him heightened a notch, and she shivered as he perused her as if he'd found the last morsel of chocolate in the pantry—and he was starving. All at once, she had a feeling they were both remembering the sweet fire of first love. They might have been young, but what they'd lacked in experience, they made up for in enthusiasm. Their relationship had hit some high notes that she'd prefer not to be remembering right this minute. Not with the man who'd made her body sing a scant few feet away.

"I haven't forgotten one day of our relationship." Why did her voice sound so breathless?

"Even the last one?" he murmured, and his voice skittered down her spine with teeth she wasn't expecting.

"I'm not sure what you mean." Confused as to why warning sirens were going off in her head, she stared at the spot where the inverted tray ceiling seams came together. "We broke up. You didn't notice. Then you joined the military and eventually came home. Here we are."

"Oh, I noticed, Grace." The honeyed quality of his tone drew her gaze to his and the green fire there blazed with heat she didn't know what to do with. "I think we can both agree that what happened between us ten years ago was a mistake. Never to be repeated. We'll let bygones be bygones and you'll figure out a way to make this pesky custody issue go away. Deal?"

A mistake. Bygones. Her heart stung as it absorbed the words that confirmed she hadn't meant that much to him. Breaking up with him hadn't fazed him the way she'd hoped. The daring ploy she'd staged to get his attention— by letting him catch her with Liam, a notorious womanizer—hadn't worked, either, because he hadn't really cared whether she messed around with his brother. The whole ruse had been for naught.

Stricken, she stared at him, unable to look away, unable to quell the turmoil inside at Kyle being close enough to touch and yet so very far away. They'd broken up ten years ago because he'd never seemed all that into their relationship. Hadn't enough time passed for her to get over it already?

"Sure. Bygones," she repeated, because that was all she could get out.

She escaped with the hasty promise that she'd send him a set schedule of home visits and drove away from Wade Ranch as fast as she dared. But she feared it would never be fast enough to catch up with her impartiality—it had scampered down the road far too quickly and she had a feeling she wasn't going to recover it. Her emotions were fully engaged in this case and she'd have to work extra hard to shut them down. So she could do the best thing for everyone. Including herself.

Kyle watched Grace drive away through the window and uncurled his fists before he punched a wall. Maybe he'd punch Liam instead.

He owed his brother one, after all, and it sure looked as though Liam was determined to be yet another roadblock in a series of roadblocks standing between Kyle and fatherhood. Most of the problems couldn't be resolved easily. But Liam wanting Kyle's kids? That was one thing that Kyle could do something about.

So he went looking for him.

Wade land surrounded the main house to the tune of about ten thousand acres. There was a time when a scouting mission like this one would have been no sweat, but with a messed-up leg, the trek winded Kyle about fifteen minutes in. Which sucked. It was tough to be sidelined, tough to reconcile no longer being in top physical condition. Tough to keep it all inside.

Kyle found Liam in the horse barn, which was situated a good half mile away from the main house. *Barn* was too simplistic a term to describe the grandiose building with a flagstone pathway to the entrance, fussy landscaping and a show arena on the far end. The ranch offices and a fancy lounge were tucked inside, but he didn't bother to gawk. His leg hurt and the walk wasn't far enough to burn off the mad Kyle had generated while talking to Grace.

Who was somehow even more beautiful than he recalled. How was that possible when he'd already put her on a pedestal in his mind as the ideal? How would any other woman ever compare? None could. And the lady herself still got him way too hot and bothered with a coy glance. It was enough to drive a man insane. She'd screwed him up so bad, he couldn't do anything other than weekend flings, like the one he'd had with Margaret. Look where that had gotten him.

Grace was a great big problem in a whole heap of problems. But not one he could deal with this minute. Liam? That was something he could handle.

He watched Liam back out of a stall housing one of the

quarter horses Wade Ranch bred commercially, waiting until his brother was clear of the door to speak. He had enough respect for the damage a spooked eleven-hundred-pound animal could do to a man to stay clear.

"What's this crap about you wanting to adopt my kids?" he said when Liam noticed him.

Liam snorted. "Grace must have come by. She tell you to sign the papers?"

No one ordered Kyle around, least of all Grace.

"She told me you've got your sights set on my family." He crossed his arms before he made good on the impulse to smash his brother in the mouth for even uttering Grace's name. She'd meant everything to Kyle, but to Liam, she was yet another in a long line of his women. "Back off. I'm taking responsibility for them whether you like it or not."

Sticking a piece of clean straw between his back teeth, Liam cocked a hip and leaned against the closed stall door as if he hadn't a care in the world. Lazily, he rearranged his battered hat. "Tell me something. What's the annual revenue Wade Ranch brings in for stud fees?"

"How should I know?" Kyle ground out. "You run the ranch."

"Yeah." Liam raised his brows sardonically. "Half of which belongs to you. Grandpa died almost two years ago, yet you've never lifted a finger to even find out what I do here. Money pours into your bank account on a monthly basis. Know how that happens? Because I make sure of it. I made sure of a lot of things while you ran around the Middle East blowing stuff up and ignoring your responsibilities at home. One of those things I do is take care of Maddie and Maggie. Because you weren't here. Just like you weren't here to take on any responsibility for the ranch. I will not let you be an absentee father like you've been an absentee ranch owner."

"That's a low blow," Kyle said softly. Liam had always

viewed Kyle's stint as a SEAL with a bit of disdain, making it clear he saw it as a cop-out. "You wanted the ranch. I didn't. But I want my girls, and I'm going to be here for them."

Wade Ranch had never meant anything to him other than a place to live because it was the only one he had. Then and now. Mama had cut and run faster than you could spit, once she'd dumped him and Liam here with her father, then taken the Dallas real estate market by storm. Lillian Wade had quickly become the Barbara Corcoran of the South and forgot all about the two little boys she'd abandoned.

Funny how Liam had been so similarly affected by dear old Mama. Enough to want to guarantee his blood wouldn't ever have to know the sting of desertion. Kyle respected the thought if not the action. But Kyle was one up on Liam, because those girls were his daughters. He wasn't about to take lessons from Mama on how to be a runaway parent.

"Too little, too late," his brother mouthed around the straw. "Hadley and I want to adopt them. I hope you have a good lawyer in your back pocket because you're not getting those girls without a hell of a fight."

God Almighty. The hits kept coming. He'd barely had time to get his feet under him from being sucker punched a minute after crossing the threshold of his childhood home, only to have Liam drop twin daughters, Grace Haines and a custody battle in his lap.

They stared at each other, neither blinking. Neither backing down. They were both stubborn enough to stand there until the cows came home, and probably would, too.

Nothing was going to get fixed this way, and with Grace's admonition to prove he was serious about providing a stable environment for Maddie and Maggie ringing in his ears, he contemplated his mule-headed brother. He wanted help with the ranch? By God, he'd get it. And

Kyle would have employment to put on his Fatherhood Résumé, which would hopefully get Grace off his back at the same time.

"Give me a job if it means so much to you that I take ranch ownership seriously. I'll do something with the horses."

Liam nearly busted a gut laughing, which did not improve Kyle's grip on his temper. "You can feed them. But that's about it. You have no training."

And Kyle wasn't at 100 percent physically, but no one had to know about that. His injuries mostly didn't count anyway. It just meant he had to work that much harder, which he'd do. Those babies were worth a little agony.

"I can learn. You can't have it both ways. Either you give me a shot at being half owner of Wade Ranch or shut up about it."

"All right, smart-ass." Liam tipped back his hat and jerked his chin at Kyle. "We got a whole cattle division here at Wade Ranch that's ripe for improvement. I've been concentrating on the horses and letting Danny and Emma Jane handle that side. You take over."

"Done."

Kyle knew even less about cows than he did babies. But he hadn't known anything about guns or explosives before joining the navy, either. BUD/S training had nearly broken him, but he'd learned how to survive impossible physical conditions, learned how to stretch his body to the point of exhaustion and still come out swinging when the next challenge reared its ugly head.

You had to start out with the mind-set that quitting wasn't an option. Even the smallest mental slip would finish a man. So he wouldn't slip.

Liam eyed him and shook his head. "You're serious?"

"As a heart attack. I'll take my best shot at the cattle side of the ranch. Just one question. What am I aiming at?"

"We have a Black Angus breeding program. Emma Jane—she's the sales manager I hired last year—is great. She sold about two hundred head. If you want me to call you successful, double that in under six months."

That didn't sound too bad, especially if there was a sales manager already doing the heavy lifting. "No problem. Now drop the whole adoption idea and we'll call it even."

"Let me see you in action, and then we'll talk. I have yet to see anything that tells me you're planning to stick around. If you take off again, the babies will be mine anyway. Might as well make it legal sooner rather than later." Liam shrugged. "You made your bed by leaving. So lie in it for a while."

Yeah, except he'd left for very specific reasons. He and Liam had never been close, and Kyle hadn't felt as if he was part of anything until he'd found his brothers of the heart on a SEAL team. That's where he'd finally felt secure. He could actually care about someone again without fear of being either abandoned or betrayed.

He'd like to say he could find a way to stay at the ranch this time. But what had changed from the first time? Not much.

Just that he was a father now. And he owed his daughters a stable home life. They were amazing little creatures that he wanted to see grow up. With the additional complications of Maddie's health problems, he couldn't relocate them at the drop of a hat, either.

"I'm not going anywhere," Kyle repeated for what felt like the four hundredth time.

Maybe if he kept saying it, people would believe him. Maybe he'd believe it, too.

Three

Kyle drove into town later that night on an errand for Hadley, who had announced at dinner that the babies were almost out of both diapers and formula. She'd seemed surprised when he said he'd go instead.

Of course he'd volunteered for the job. They were his kids. But he'd made Hadley write down exactly what he needed to buy, because the only formula he'd had exposure to was the one for making homemade explosives. List in his pocket, he'd swung into his truck, intending to grab the baby items and be back in jiffy.

But as he pulled into the lot at Royal's one-and-only grocery store, Grace had just exited through the automatic sliding doors. Well, well, well. There was no way he was passing up this opportunity. He still had a boatload of questions for the girl he'd once given his heart to, only to have it handed back, shredded worse than Black Angus at a slaughterhouse.

Kyle waited until she was almost to her car, and then

gingerly climbed from his truck to corner her between her Toyota and the Dooley in the next spot.

"Lovely night, isn't it, Ms. Haines?"

She jumped and spun around, bobbling her plastic sack full of her grocery store purchases. "You scared me."

"Guilty conscience maybe," he offered silkily. No time like the present to give her a chance to own up to the crimes she'd committed so long ago. He might even forgive her if she just said she was sorry.

"No, more like I'm a woman in a dark parking lot and I hear a man speaking to me unexpectedly."

It was a perfectly legitimate thing to say except the streetlight spilled over her face, illuminating her scowl and negating her point about a dark parking lot. She was that bent up about him saying *hey* outside of a well-lit grocery store?

He raised a brow. "This is Royal. The most danger you'd find in the parking lot of the HEB is a runaway shopping cart."

"You've been gone a long time, Kyle. Things have changed."

Yeah, more than he'd have liked. Grace's voice had deepened. It was far sexier than he'd recalled, and he'd thought about her a lot. Her curves were lusher, as if she'd gained a few pounds in all the right places, and he had an unexpected urge to pull her against him so he could explore every last change, hands on.

Okay, the way he constantly wanted her? *That* was still the same. He'd always been crazy over her. She'd been an exercise in patience, making him wait until they'd been dating a year *and* she'd turned eighteen before she'd sleep with him the first time. And that had been so mind-blowing, he'd immediately started working on the second encounter, then the third. And so on.

The fact that he'd fallen in love with her along the way

was the craziest thing. He didn't make it a habit to let people in. She'd been an exception, one he hadn't been able to help.

"You haven't changed," he said without thinking. "You're still the prettiest girl in the whole town."

Now why had he gone and said something like that? Just because it was true didn't mean he should run off at the mouth. Last thing he needed was to give her the slightest opening. She'd slide right under his skin again, just as she'd done the first time, as if his barriers against people who might hurt him didn't exist.

"Flattery?" She rolled her eyes. "That was a lame line. Plus, I already told you I'd handle your case impartially. There's no point in trying to butter me up."

Oh, so she thought she was immune to his charm, did she? He grinned and shifted his weight off his bad leg, cocking his right hip out casually as if he'd meant to strike that stance all along. "I wouldn't dream of it. That was the God-honest truth. I've been around the world, and I know a thing or two about attractive women. No law against telling one so."

"Well, I don't like it. Are you really that clueless, Kyle?"

The scowl crawled back onto her face and it tripped his Spidey-sense. Or at least that's what he'd always called it. He'd discovered in SEAL training that he had no small amount of skill in reading a situation or a person. Before then, he'd spent a lot of time by himself—purposefully— and never paid much attention to people's tells. Honing that ability had served him well in hostile territory.

So he could easily see Grace was mad. At *him*.

What was that all about? She was the one who'd dumped him cold with no explanation other than she wanted to concentrate on school, which was bull. She'd been a straight-A student before they'd started dating and maintained her grade point average until the day she graduated a year after he had. Best he could figure, she'd wanted Liam instead and hadn't wasted any time getting with his brother once she was free and clear.

"You got something to say, Grace?" He crossed his arms and leaned against her four-door sedan. "Seems like you got a bee in your bonnet."

Maybe Liam had thrown her over too quickly and she'd lumped her hurt feelings into a big Wade bucket. And now he was giving her a second shot to spill it. He just wanted her to admit she'd hurt him and then say she was sorry. That she'd picked the wrong brother when she'd hooked up with Liam. Then maybe he could go on and meet someone new and exciting who didn't constantly remind him that Kyle, women and relationships didn't mix well. Maybe he'd even find a way to trust a woman again. He could finally move on from Grace Haines.

She licked her lips and stared at the sky over his shoulder. "I'm sorry. I'm not handling this well. The babies are important to me. All my cases are, but because we used to date, I want to ensure there's no hint of impropriety. All the decisions I make should be based on facts and your ability to provide a good home. So please don't say things like you think I'm pretty."

Something that felt a lot like disappointment whacked him between the eyes. She had yet to mention the episode with Liam. Maybe she didn't even know that Kyle had seen them together, or didn't care. No, he'd never said anything to her about it, either, because some things should be obvious. You didn't fool around with a guy's brother. It was a universal law and if he had to spell that out, Grace wasn't as great a girl as he'd always thought.

"Well, then," Kyle said easily. "Maybe you should transfer my case to someone else in the county, so you don't have to deal with my brand of truth."

She probably didn't even remember what she'd done

with Liam and most likely thought Kyle had moved on. He *should* have moved on. It was way past time.

She shook her head. "Can't. We're overloaded. So we're stuck with each other."

Which meant she'd checked into it. That was somehow more disappointing than her skipping over the apology he was owed.

No matter.

Grace was just a woman he used to date. That's all. There was nothing between them any longer. He'd spent years shutting down everything inside and he'd keep on doing it. Nothing new here.

And she had his babies and their future in the palm of her hand. This was the one person he needed on his side. They could both stand to act like adults about this situation and focus on what was good for the children. It would be a good idea to do exactly as he suggested to her and let bygones be bygones. Even though he hadn't meant a word of it at the time.

"You're right. I'm sorry, too. Let's start over, friendly-like." He held out his hand for her to shake.

She hesitated for an eternity and then reached out to take it.

The contact sang through his palm, setting off all kinds of fireworks in places that had been cold and dark for a really long time. Gripping his hand tight, she met his gaze and held it.

The depths of her brown eyes heated, melting a little of the ice in his heart.

Her mouth would be sweet under his, and her skin would be soft and fragrant. The moon had risen, spilling silver light over the parking lot, and the gentle breeze played with her hair. The atmosphere couldn't be more romantic if he'd ordered it up. He barely resisted yanking her into his arms.

Yeah, he was in a lot of trouble if he was supposed to keep this friendly and impartial. She was his babies' caseworker. But the fact of the matter was that he had never gotten over Grace Haines. He could no sooner shut down his feelings about her than he could pick up her Toyota with one hand. And being around her again was pure torture.

The next morning, Kyle woke at dawn the way he always did. He'd weaned himself off an alarm clock about two weeks into BUD/S training and hadn't ever gone back.

He lay there staring at the ceiling of his old room at Wade House. Reorientation time. *Not a SEAL. Not in Afghanistan. Not in the hospital*—which had been its own kind of nightmare. This was the hardest part of the day. Every morning, he took stock, so he'd know who and where he was. Then he thanked God for the opportunity to serve his country and cursed the evil that had required it.

This was also the time of day when he made the decision to leave the pain pills in the bottle, where they belonged.

Some days, that decision was tougher than others. There was a deep, dark place inside that craved the oblivion the drugs would surely bring. That's why he'd never cracked open the seal on the bottle. Too easy to have a mental slip and think *just this once*. That was cheating, and Kyle had never taken that route.

Today would not mark the start of it, either.

Today did mark the start of something, though. A new kind of taking stock about the things he was instead of the things he wasn't. *A father. A cattle rancher*. He liked the sound of that. It was nice to have some positives to call out. He needed positives after six months of hell.

Of course, Grace would be watching over his shoulder, and Liam was going to be smack in the middle of Kyle's steps toward fatherhood *and* ranching. The two people he distrusted the most and both held the keys to his future.

He rolled from bed and pulled on a new long-sleeved shirt, jeans and boots. Eventually, his wardrobe would be work-worn like Liam's, but for now, he'd have to settle for looking like a rhinestone cowboy instead of a real one. Coffee beckoned, so he took the back stairway from the third floor to the ground floor kitchen, albeit a bit more slowly than he'd have liked.

Hadley had beaten him to the coffeepot and turned with a smile when he entered. "Good morning. Sleep well?"

"Fine," he lied. He'd lain awake far too long thinking about how this woman and his brother wanted to take his kids away. "And you?"

"Great. The babies only woke up once and thankfully at the same time. It's not always like that. Sometimes they wake up all night long at intervals." She laughed good-naturedly and lowered her voice. "I think they plan it out ahead of time just to make me nuts."

Guilt crushed Kyle's lungs and he struggled to breathe. Some father he was. They'd agreed the night before that Hadley would continue in her role as Maddie and Maggie's caretaker until Kyle got his feet under him, but it didn't feel any more right this morning than it had then. His sister-in-law was getting up in the middle of the night with his kids, scant hours after he gave Liam and Grace a big speech about how he was all prepared to step up and provide a loving environment.

No more.

"I appreciate what you're doing for my daughters," he rasped, and cleared his throat. "But I want to take care of them from now on. I'll get up with them at night."

Hadley stared at him. "You have no idea what you're talking about, do you?"

"Uh, well…" Should he brazen it out or admit defeat?

God Almighty, he hated admitting any kind of weakness. But chances were good she'd already figured out he wasn't the brightest bulb on the board when it came to babies. "I'm going to learn. Trial by fire is how I operate best."

"They're not going to pull out AK-47s, Kyle." Hadley hid a smile but not very well and handed him a cup of steaming coffee. "Sugar and creamer are on the table."

"I like it black, thanks." He sipped and added *good coffee* to his list of things he was thankful for. "Tell me the things I need to know about my kids."

"Okay." She nodded and went over a list of basics, which Kyle committed to memory. Eating. Bathing. Sleeping. Check, check, check. Stuff all humans needed, but his little humans couldn't do these things for themselves. He just had to help them, the way he would a wounded teammate.

"Can I see them?" he asked. Felt weird to be asking permission, but he didn't want to mess up anything.

"You can. They're sleeping, but we can sneak in. You can be quiet, right?"

"Quiet enough to take out a barracks full of enemy soldiers without getting caught," he said without a trace of irony. Hadley just smiled as though he was kidding.

He followed Hadley to the nursery, a mysterious place full of pink and tiny beds with bars. The girls were asleep in their cribs, and he watched them for a moment, his throat tight. Their little faces—how could anything be that tiny and survive? A better question was, how did your heart stay stitched together when it felt as if it would burst from all the stuff swelling up inside it?

"I was their nanny first, you know," she whispered. "Before I married Liam."

What did a nanny even do? Was she like a babysitter and a substitute mom all rolled up into one? If so, that seemed like a bonus, and he'd be cutting off his nose to spite his face to relieve her of her duties. She could keep on being the nanny as far as he was concerned, as long as Grace was okay with it. She must be. Liam had hired Hadley, after all, and Grace seemed pretty impressed with them as a team.

"I'm not trying to take away your job," he mumbled.

Did she see it as a job? If she and Liam wanted to adopt the girls, she'd obviously grown very attached to them. Was it better to cut off their contact with the babies instead? Get them used to the idea?

If so, he couldn't do it. It seemed unnecessarily cruel and besides, he needed the help.

"I didn't think you were. It's admirable that you want to care for them, but there's a huge learning curve and they won't do well with a big disruption. Let's take it one step at a time."

He could do that. You didn't drop a green recruit into the middle of a Taliban hotbed and expect him to wipe out the insurgents as his first assignment. You started him out with something simple, like surveillance. "Can I watch you feed them?"

"Sure, when they wake up."

They tiptoed from the room and Kyle considered that a pretty successful start to Operation: Fatherhood.

Next up, Operation: Do Something About Grace. Because he'd lain awake last night thinking about her more than he'd wanted to, as well. Somehow, he had to shut down the spark between them. Or hose it off with a big, wet kiss.

Grace sat in her car outside of Wade House and pretended that she was going over some notes in her case file. In truth, her stomach was doing a cancan at the prospect of seeing Kyle again, and she couldn't get it to settle.

She'd gone a long time without seeing him. What was so different now?

Nothing. She was a professional and she would do her job. *Get out of the car*, she admonished herself. *Get in there and do your assessment.* The faster she gathered the facts needed to remove the babies from Kyle's presence and provide a recommendation for their permanent home, the better.

Hadley let her into the house and directed her to the second floor, where Kyle was hanging out with the babies. Perfect. She could watch him interact with them and record some impartial observations in her files.

But when Grace poked her head into the nursery with a bright smile, it died on her face. Kyle dozed in the rocking chair, Maddie against one shoulder, Maggie the other. Both babies were asleep, swaddled in soft pink blankets, an odd contrast to Kyle's masculine attire.

But that wasn't the arresting part. It was Kyle. Unguarded, vulnerable. Sweet even, with his large hands cradled protectively around each of his daughters. He should look ridiculous in the middle of a nursery decorated to the nth degree with girlie colors and baby items. But he looked anything but. His powerful body scarcely fit into the rocking chair, biceps and broad shoulders spilling past the edges of the back. He'd always been incredibly handsome, but on the wiry side.

No more. He was built like a tank, and she could easily imagine this man taking out any threat in a mile-wide radius.

It was a lot more affecting than she would ever admit.

And then his eyelids blinked open. He didn't move a muscle otherwise, but his keen gaze zeroed in on her. Fully alert. Those hard green eyes cut through her, leaving her feeling exposed and much more aware of Kyle than she'd been a minute ago. Which was saying something, given her thoughts had already been pretty graphic.

It was heady to be in his sights like that. He'd always

looked at her as if they shared something special that no one else could or would be involved in. But he'd honed his focus over the years into something new and razor sharp. Flustered, she wiggled her fingers in a half wave, and that's when he smiled.

It hit her in the soft part of her heart and spread a warmth she did not want to feel. But oh, my, it was delicious. Like when he'd taken her hand in the parking lot last night. That feeling—she'd missed it.

She'd lain awake last night imagining that he'd kissed her the way she'd have sworn he wanted to as they stood under that streetlight. It was all wrong between them. Kissing wasn't allowed, wasn't part of the agenda, wasn't what should happen. But it didn't stop her from thinking about it.

She was in a lot of trouble.

"Hi," she murmured, because she felt that she had to say something instead of standing there ogling a gorgeous man as he rocked his infant daughters against an explosion of pink.

"Hi," he mouthed back. "Is it time for our visit already?"

She nodded. "I can come back."

She didn't move as he gave a slight shake of his head. Carefully, he peeled his body from the chair, not jostling even one hair on the head of his precious bundles. As if he'd done it a million times, he laid first one, then the other in their cribs. Neither one woke.

It was a sight to see.

He turned and tiptoed toward the door, but she hadn't moved from her frozen stance in the doorway yet. She should move.

But he stopped right there in front of her, a half smile lingering on his lips as he laid a hand on her arm, presumably to usher her from the room ahead of him. His palm was warm and her skin tingled under it. The feeling threatened to engulf her whole body in a way that she hadn't been *engulfed* in a long time.

Not since Kyle.

Goodness, it seemed so ridiculous, but the real reason it hadn't been hard to stop dating was because no one compared. She was almost thirty and had only had one lover in her life—this man before her with the sparkling green eyes and beautiful face. And she'd take that secret to the grave.

Her cheeks heated as she imagined admitting such a thing to a guy who had likely cut a wide swath through the eligible women beating a path to his door. He hadn't let the grass grow under his feet, now, had he? Fathering twins with a woman he'd written off soon after spoke loudly enough to that question.

If she told him, he'd mistakenly assume she still had feelings for him, and that wasn't exactly true. She just couldn't find a man who fit her stringent criteria for intimacy. Call it old-fashioned, but she wanted to be in love before making love. And most men weren't willing to be that patient.

Except Kyle. He'd never uttered one single complaint when he found out she wasn't hopping into his bed after a few weeks of dating. And oh, my, had it been worth the wait.

The heat in her cheeks spread, and the tingles weren't just under his palm. No, they were a good bit more in a region where she shouldn't be getting so hot, especially not over Kyle and his brand-new warrior's body, laser-sharp focus and gentle hands.

Mercy, she should stop thinking about all that. Except he was looking at her the way he had last night, gaze on her lips, and she wondered if he'd actually do it this time— kiss her as he had so many times before.

One of the babies yowled and the moment broke into pieces.

Kyle's expression instantly morphed into one of concern as he spun toward the crib of the crying infant. Maddie. It was easy to tell them apart if you knew she was the smaller of the two girls. She'd worn a heart monitor for a long time but Grace didn't see the telltale wires poking out of the baby's tiny outfit. Hopefully that meant the multiple surgeries had been successful.

"Hey, now. What's all this fuss?" he murmured, and scooped up the bundle of pink, holding her to his shoulder with rocking motions.

The baby cried harder. Lines of frustration popped up around Kyle's mouth as he kept trying different positions against his shoulder, rocking harder, then slower.

"You liked this earlier," he said. "I'm following procedure here, little lady. Give me a break."

Grace hid a smile. "Maybe her diaper is wet."

Kyle nodded and strode to the changing table. "One diaper change, coming up."

He pulled a diaper from the drawer under the table, laid the baby on the foam pad, then tied the holding straps designed to keep Maddie from rolling to the ground with intricate knots. Next, he lined up the baby powder and diaper rash cream, determination rolling from him in thick waves. When the man put his mind to something, it was dizzying to watch.

With precision, he stripped the baby out of her onesie and took a swift kick to the wrist with good humor as he changed her diaper. It didn't help. The baby wailed a little louder.

"No problem," he said. "Babies usually cry for three reasons. They want to be held. Diaper. And…" A line appeared between Kyle's brows.

Then Maggie woke up and cried in harmony with her sister.

"Want me to pick her up?" Grace asked.

"No. I can handle this. Don't count me out yet." He nestled the other baby into his arms, rocking both with little murmurs. "Bottle. That was the other one Hadley said. We'll try eating."

Bless his heart. He'd gone to Hadley for baby lessons. He was trying so hard, much harder than she'd expected. It warmed her in a whole different way than the sizzle a moment ago. And the swell in her heart was much more dangerous.

The bottle did the trick. After Kyle got both girls fed, they quieted down and fell back asleep in their cribs. This time, he and Grace made it out of the room, but when they reached the living area off the kitchen, *flustered* was too kind a word for the state of her nerves.

Kyle collapsed on the couch with a groan.

"So," she croaked after taking a seat as far away from him as possible. "That was pretty stressful."

"Nah." He scrubbed his face with his hand and peeked out through his fingers. "Stressful is dismantling a home-made pipe bomb before it kills someone."

They'd never talked about his life in the military—largely because he was so closemouthed about it—and judging from the shadows she glimpsed in his expression sometimes, the experience hadn't softened him up any, that was for sure. "Is that what you did overseas? Handle explosives?"

Slowly, he nodded. "That was my specialty, yeah."

He could have died. Easily. A hundred times over, and she'd probably never have known until they paraded his flag-draped coffin through the streets of Royal. The thought was upsetting in a way she really didn't understand, which only served to heighten her already-precarious emotional state.

He'd been serving his country, not using the military as an excuse to stay away. The realization swept through her, blowing away some of her anger and leaving in its place a bit of guilt over never acknowledging his sacrifices in the name of liberty.

"And now you're ready to buckle down and be a father."

It seemed ludicrous. This powerful, strapping man wanted to trade bombs for babies. But when she recalled the finesse he used when handling the babies, she couldn't deny that he had a delicate touch.

"I do what needs to be done," he said quietly, and his green eyes radiated sincerity that she couldn't quite look away from.

When had Kyle become so responsible? Such an *adult*? He was different in such baffling, subtle ways that she kept stumbling in her quest to objectively assess his fitness as a parent.

"Did you give any thought to our discussion yesterday?" she asked.

"The job? I signed on to head up Wade Ranch's cattle division. How's that for serious?"

Kyle leaned back against the couch cushions, looking much more at home in this less formal area than he'd been in the Victorian parlor yesterday, and crossed one booted foot over his knee. Cowboy boots, not the military-issue black boots he'd been wearing yesterday. It was a small detail, but a telling one.

He'd quietly transitioned roles when she wasn't looking. Could it mean he'd been telling the truth when he'd said he planned to stay this time?

"It's a start," she said simply, but that didn't begin to describe what was actually starting.

She'd have to adjust every last thing she'd ever thought about Kyle Wade and his ability to be a father. And if she did, she might also have to think about him differently in a lot of other respects as well, such as whether or not he'd grown up enough to become her everything once again. But this time forever.

Four

Kyle reported to the Wade Ranch cattle barn for duty at zero dark thirty. At least he'd remembered to refer to the beasts as cattle instead of cows. Slowly but surely, snippets of his youth had started coming back to him as he'd driven to the barn. He'd watched his grandfather, Calvin Wade, manage the ranch for years. Kyle remembered perching on the top rail of the cattle pen while Calvin branded the calves or helped Doc Glade with injured cows.

Things had changed significantly since then. The cattle barn had been rebuilt and relocated a half mile from the main house. It was completely separate from the horse business, and Liam's lack of interest in the cattle side couldn't have been clearer. His brother had even hired a ranch manager.

Kyle could practically hear the rattle of Grandpa rolling over in his grave.

He'd always insisted that a man had to manage his own business and Calvin hadn't had much respect for "gentleman" ranchers who spent their money on women and whiskey and hired other men to do the work of running the ranch. Clearly Liam hadn't agreed.

The red barn dominated the clearing ahead. A long empty pen ran along the side of the building. The cattle must be roaming. Kyle parked his truck in a lot near a handful of other vehicles with the Wade Ranch logo on the doors. Easing from the cab, he hit the ground with bated breath. So far, so good. The cowboy boots were a little stiff and the heel put his leg at a weird angle, but he was going to ignore all that as long as possible.

He strolled to the barn, which had an office similar to the one in the horse barn. But that's where the similarities ended. This was a working barn, complete with the smell of manure and hay. Kyle had smelled a lot worse. It reminded him of Grandpa, and there was something nice about following in Calvin's footsteps. They'd never been close, but then Kyle had never been close with anyone. Except Grace.

The ranch manager, Danny Spencer, watched Kyle approach and spat on the ground as he contemplated his new boss.

"You pick out a horse yet, son?"

Kyle's hackles rose. He was no one's son, least of all this man who was maybe fifteen years his senior. It was a deliberate choice of phrasing designed to put Kyle in his place. Wasn't going to work. "First day on the job."

"We ride here. You skedaddle on over to the other barn and come back on a horse. Then we'll talk."

It felt like a test and Kyle intended to pass. So he climbed back into his truck and drove to the horse barn. He felt like a mama's boy driving. But he was in a hurry to get started and walking wasn't one of his skills right now.

Maybe one day.

Liam was already at the barn, favoring an early start

as well, apparently. He helped Kyle find a suitable mount without one smart-alecky comment, which did not go unnoticed. Kyle just chose not to say anything about it.

A few ranch hands gathered to watch, probably hoping Kyle would bust his ass a couple of times and they could video it with their cell phones. He wondered what they'd been told about Kyle's return. Did everyone know about the babies and Margaret's death?

Sucker's bet. Of course they did. Wade Ranch was its own kind of small town. Didn't matter. Kyle was the boss, whether they liked it or not. Whether he had the slightest clue what he was doing. Or not.

The horse didn't like him any better than Danny Spencer did. When he stuck a boot in the stirrup, the animal tried to dance sideways and would have bucked him off if Kyle hadn't kept a tight grip on the pommel. "Hey, now. Settle down."

Liam had called the horse Lightning Rod. Dumb name. But it was all Kyle had.

"That's a good boy, Lightning Rod." It seemed to calm the dark brown quarter horse somewhat, so Kyle tried to stick his boot in the stirrup again. This time, he ended up in the saddle, which felt just as foreign as everything else on the ranch did.

The ranch hands applauded sarcastically, mumbling to each other. He almost apologized for ruining their fun— also sarcastically—but he let it go.

Somehow, Kyle managed to get up to a trot as he rode out onto the trail back to the cattle barn. It had been a lifetime since he'd ridden a horse and longer than that since he'd wanted to.

God, everything hurt. The trot was more of a trounce, and he longed for the bite of rock under his belly as he dismantled a homemade cherry bomb placed carefully under a mosque where three hundred people worshipped. That he understood at least. How he'd landed in the middle of a job managing cattle, he didn't.

Oh, right. He was doing this to prove to everyone they were wrong about him. That he wasn't a slacker who'd ignored messages about his flesh and blood. That Liam and Grace and Danny Spencer and everyone else who had a bone to pick with him weren't going to make him quit.

When he got back to the cattle barn, Danny and the cattle hands were hanging around waiting. One of the disappointed guys from the horse barn had probably texted ahead, hoping someone else could get video of the boss falling off his mount. They could all keep being disappointed.

"One cattle rancher on a horse, as ordered," Kyle called mildly, keeping his ire under wraps. Someone wanted to know what he really thought about things? Too bad. No one was privy to what went on inside Kyle's head except Kyle. As always.

"That'll do," Danny said with a nod, but his scowl didn't loosen up any. "We got a few hundred head in the north pasture that need to be rounded up. You take Slim and Johnny and ya'll bring 'em back, hear?"

"Nothing wrong with my ears," Kyle drawled lazily. "What's wrong is that I'm the one calling the shots now. What do you say we chat about that for a bit?"

Danny spat on the ground near Lighting Rod's left front hoof and the horse flicked his head back in response. Kyle choked up on the reins before his mount got the brilliant idea to bolt.

"I'd say you started drinking early this a.m. if you think you're calling the shots, jarhead."

Kyle let loose a wry chuckle, friendly like, so no one got the wrong idea. "You might want to brush up on your insults. Jarheads are marines, not SEALs."

"Same thing."

Neither of them blinked as Kyle grinned. "Nah. The marines let anyone in, even old cowhands with bad attitudes. Want me to pass your number on to a recruiter? I'll let you go a couple of rounds with a drill sergeant, and when you come back, you can talk to me about the difference between marines and SEALs all you want. Until then, my last name is Wade and the only thing you're permitted to call me is 'boss.'"

Spencer didn't flinch but neither did he nod and play along. He spun on his heel and disappeared into the barn with a backhanded wave. Kyle considered it a win that the man hadn't flipped him a one-fingered salute as a bonus.

Now that the unpleasantness was out of the way, Kyle nodded at the two hands the ranch manager had singled out as his lieutenants, one of whom had fifty pounds on him. That one must be Slim. It was the kind of joke cowboys seemed to like. Kyle would probably be *jarhead* until the day he died after a recounting of his showdown with Danny Spencer made the gossip rounds.

"You boys have a problem working for me?" he asked them both.

Slim's expression was nothing short of hostile, but he and Johnny both shook their heads and swung up on their horses, trotting obediently after Kyle as he headed north toward the pasture where the cattle he was supposed to herd were grazing.

Then he just needed to figure out how to do it. Without alienating anyone else. Oh, and without falling off his horse. And without letting on to anyone that his leg was on fire already after less than thirty minutes in the saddle.

The north pasture came into view. Finally. It was still exactly where it had been ten years ago, but it felt as though it had taken a million years to get there, especially given the tense silence between Kyle and the two hands. Cattle dotted the wide swath of Wade land like black shadows against the green grass, spread as far as the eye could see, even wandering aimlessly into a copse of trees in the distance.

That was not good. He'd envisioned the cattle being easy to round up because they were all more or less in the same place. Instead, he and the hands had a very long task ahead of them to gather up the beasts, who may or may not have wanted to be gathered.

"How many?" he called over his shoulder to Johnny.

"A few hundred." Johnny repeated verbatim the vague number Danny Spencer had rattled off earlier.

He'd mellowed out some and had actually spoken to Kyle without growling. Slim, not so much. The man held a serious grudge that wouldn't be easily remedied. No big thing. They didn't have to like each other. Just work together.

"How many exactly?" Kyle asked again as patiently as possible. "We have to know if we have them all before we head back."

Johnny looked at him cockeyed as if Kyle had started speaking in tongues and thrown around a couple of snakes in the baptismal on a Sunday morning. "We just round 'em up and aim toward the barn. Nothing more to it than that."

"Maybe not before. But today, we're going to make sure we have full inventory before we make the trek." Kyle couldn't do it more than once. There was no way. "Liam didn't happen to invest in GPS, did he?"

Slim and Johnny exchanged glances. "Uh…what?"

"Satellite. RFID chips. You embed the chips in the cow's brand, for example, and use a GPS program to triangulate the chips. Technology to locate and count cattle." At the blank looks he received in response, Kyle gave up. "I'll take that as a no."

That would be Kyle's first investment as head of the cattle division at Wade Ranch. RFID chips would go a long way toward inventorying livestock that ran tame across hundreds of acres. That was how the military kept track of soldiers and supplies, after all. Seemed like a no-brainer to do the same with valuable livestock. He wondered why Liam hadn't done it already.

"All right, then." Kyle sighed. "Let's do this."

The three men rode hard for a couple of hours, driving the cattle toward the gate, eventually feeling confident that they had them all. Kyle had to accept the eyeball guesstimate from Slim and Johnny, who had "done this a couple of times." Both thought the number of bodies seemed about right. Since Kyle wasn't experienced enough to argue, he nodded and let the experts guide them home.

It was exhausting and invigorating at the same time. This was his land. His cattle. His men, despite the lack of welcome.

But when he got back to the cattle barn, Liam was waiting for him, arms crossed and a livid expression on his face.

"What now?" Kyle slid from his horse, keeping a tight grip on the pommel until he was sure his leg would support him.

"Danny Spencer quit." Liam fairly spat. "And walked out without even an hour's notice. Said he'd rather eat manure than work for you. Nice going."

"That's the best news I've heard all day." God's honest truth. The relief was huge. "He doesn't want to work for me? Fine. Better that he's gone."

Liam pulled Kyle away from the multitude of hands swarming the area by the barn, probably all with perked-up ears, hoping to catch more details about the unfolding drama.

"It's not better," Liam muttered darkly. "Are you out of your mind? You can't come in here and throw your weight around. Danny's been handling the cattle side. I told you that. This is his territory and you came in and upset the status quo in less than five minutes."

Kyle shook his head. "Not his territory anymore. It's mine."

"Seriously?" Liam's snort was half laugh and half frustration. "You don't get it. These men respect Danny. Follow him. They don't like you. What are you going to do if they all quit? You can't run a cattle division by yourself."

Yeah, but he'd rather try than put up with dissension in the ranks. Catering to the troops was the fastest way to give the enemy an advantage. There could only be one guy in charge, and it was Kyle. "They can all quit then. There are plenty of ranch hands in this area. I need men who will work, not drama queens all bent out of shape because a bigger fish swam into their pond."

"Fine." Liam threw up his hands. "You have at it. Don't say I didn't warn you. Just keep in mind that we have a deal."

His brother stomped to his truck and peeled out of the clearing with a spray of rock. Kyle resisted the urge to wave, mostly because Liam was probably too pissed to look in his rearview mirror and also because the hands were eyeing him with scowls. No point in being cocky on top of clueless.

His girls were worth whatever he had to do to figure this out.

Johnny approached him then. Kyle had just about had enough of cattle, his aching leg, difficult ranch managers and a hardheaded brother.

"What?" he snapped.

"Uh, I just wanted to tell you thanks." Johnny cleared his throat. "For your service to the country."

The genuine sentiment pierced Kyle through the stomach. And nearly put him on the ground where a day of hard riding hadn't. It was the first time anyone in Royal had positively acknowledged his time in the military. Not that he'd been expecting a three-piece band and a parade. He'd rather stay out of the spotlight—that kind of welcome was for true heroes, not a guy who'd gotten on the wrong end of a bullet.

Nonetheless, Kyle's bad day didn't seem so bad anymore.

"Yeah," he said gruffly. "You're welcome. You know someone who served?"

Usually, the only people who thought about thanking veterans were those with family or friends in the armed forces. It was just a fact. Regular people enjoyed their freedom well enough but rarely thought about the people behind the sacrifices required to secure it.

Johnny nodded, his eyes wide and full of grief. "My dad. He was killed in the first Gulf War. I was still a baby. I never got to know him."

Ouch. That was the kicker. No matter what else, Kyle and this kid had a bond that could never be broken.

Kyle simply held out his hand and waited until Johnny grasped it. "That's a shame. I'm sorry for your loss. I stood in for great fallen men like your dad and helped continue the job he started. I'm proud I got to follow in his footsteps."

The younger man shook his hand solemnly, and then there was nothing more to say. Some things didn't need words.

Kyle hit the shower when he got back to the house. When he emerged, Liam and Hadley asked if they could take the babies for a walk in their double stroller before dinner, and would he like to come?

A walk. They might as well have asked if he'd like to fly. He'd have a hard time with a crawl at this point. After the fishhooks Johnny had sunk into his heart, he'd rather be alone anyway, though it killed him to be unable to do something as simple as push his daughters in a stroller. He waved Liam and his new wife off with a smile, hoped it came across as sincere and limped into the family room to watch something inane on TV.

There was a halfway decent World War II documentary on the History Channel that caught his interest. He watched it for a few minutes until the doorbell rang.

"That was fast," he said as he yanked open the door with a grin he'd dare anyone to guess was fake, expecting to see Liam and Hadley with chagrined expressions because they'd forgotten their key.

But it was Grace. Beautiful, fresh-faced Grace, who stood on the porch with clasped hands, long brown hair down her back, wearing a long-sleeved sweater with form-fitting jeans. It was a hard to peel his eyes from her. But he did. Somehow.

"Hey, Kyle," she said simply.

His smile became real instantly. Why, he couldn't say. Grace was still a bundle of trouble tied up with a big old impossible knot. But where was the fun in leaving a tangle alone?

They'd agreed to forget about the past and start over. But they hadn't fully established what they were starting, at least not to his satisfaction. Maybe now would be a good time to get that straight.

"Hey, Grace." He crossed his arms and leaned on the door frame, cocking his busted leg to take the weight off. "What can I do for you?"

The sun shone behind her, close to setting for the day, spilling fiery reds and yellows into the deep crevices of the sky. As backdrops went, it wasn't half-bad. But it wasn't nearly as spectacular as the woman.

"We had an appointment. Earlier."

Kyle swore. He'd totally forgotten. Wasn't that just

dandy? Made him look like a stellar father to blow off his daughters' caseworker.

Fix it. He needed Grace's good favor.

"But you were off doing cowboy things," she continued. Her voice had grown a little breathy as if she'd run to the door from her car. But the scant distance between here and there sure didn't account for the pink spreading through her cheeks.

"Yep. Someone advised me I might want to find permanent employment if I hoped to be a daddy to my girls. Sorry I missed you." He raised a brow. "But it's mighty accommodating of you to reschedule, considering. 'Preciate it."

Good thing she hadn't wandered down to the barn so she could witness firsthand his impressive debut as the boss.

"No problem," she allowed. "I have to do the requisite number of site visits before I make my recommendations and I do want to be thorough."

Maybe there was room to get her mind off her recommendations and on to something a little more pleasant. *Before* she made any snap judgments about his ability to recall a small thing like an appointment with the person who had the most power to screw up his life. Well, actually, Grace was probably second, behind Kyle—if there was anyone who got the honor of being an A1 screwup thus far in this custody issue, it was him.

"Why don't we sit for a minute?" He gestured to the porch rocker to the left of the front door, which had a great view of the sunset. Might as well put Liam's revamp of the house to good use, and do some reconnaissance at the same time. Grace had to provide a report with her recommendations. He got that. But he wanted to know more about the woman providing the report than anything else at this moment.

"Oh." She glanced at the rocker and then over his shoulder into the interior of the house. "It would probably be best if I watched you interact with the girls again. Like yesterday. That's the quickest way for me to see what kind of environment you'll provide."

"That would be great. Except they aren't here. Liam and Hadley took them for a walk before dinner." Quickly, before she could ask why he hadn't joined them, he held up a finger as if a brilliant idea had just occurred to him. "Why don't you stay and eat with us? You can see how the Wade family handles meals. Meanwhile, we can hang out on the porch and wait for them to get back."

"Um…"

He closed the front door and hustled her over to the bench seat with a palm to the small of her back. To be fair, she didn't resist too much and willingly sank into the rocker, but as soon as he sat next to her, it became clear that *he* should have been the one resisting.

The essence of Grace spilled over him as they got cozy in the two-seater. It was too small for someone his size and their hips snugged up against each other. The contact burned through his jeans, sensitizing his skin, and as he tried to ease off a bit, his foot hit the porch board and set the rocker in motion. Which only knocked her against him more firmly so that her amazing breasts grazed his arm.

Actually, the rocker was exactly the right size for Kyle and Grace. Sitting in it with her might have been the best idea he'd ever had in his life.

Her fresh, spring-like scent wound through his head. They'd sat like this at her mama's house, but in the living room while pretending to watch TV on a Saturday night. It passed for a date in a place like Royal, where teenagers could either get in trouble sneaking around the football stadium with filched beer or hang out under the watchful eye of the folks. Usually Kyle and Grace had opted for the latter, at least until her parents went to bed. Then they got down to some serious making out.

He'd never been as affected by a woman as he'd been by this one. Even just a kiss could knock him for a loop. The memories of how good it had been washed through him, blasting away some of the darkness that had taken over inside. She'd always been so eager. So pliant under his mouth.

All at once, he wondered if she still tasted the same, like innocence laced with a warm breeze.

"Grace," he murmured. Somehow his arm had snaked across the back of the rocker, closing the small gap between them.

Grace's brown eyes peeked out underneath her lashes as she watched him for a moment. Maybe she was wondering the same. If that spark would still be there after all this time.

"How long will it be until Liam and Hadley are back with the girls?" she asked, her voice low.

"Later. Don't worry. We won't miss them."

"I, uh…wasn't worried."

She licked her lips, drawing his attention to her mouth, and suddenly that was all he could see. All he could think about. Her lips had filled out, along with the rest of her face. She'd grown into a woman while he'd been away, with some interesting new experiences shining in her eyes.

All at once, he wanted to know what they were.

"I've been wondering," he said. "Why did you become a social worker? I seem to recall you wanted to be a schoolteacher way back."

That was not what he'd meant to ask. But she lit up at the question. And the sunset? Not even a blip in his consciousness. Her face had all the warmth a man would ever need.

"I did. Want to," she clarified. "That's what I majored in. But I went to do my student teaching and something just didn't work right. The students weren't the problem. Oh, they were a bit unruly but they were fourth graders. You gotta expect some ants in the pants. It was me. There was no...click. You know what I mean?"

"Yeah." He nodded immediately. Like when he hit his stride in BUD/S training on the second day and knew he'd found his place in the world. "Then what happened?"

"I volunteered some places for a while. Tried to get my feet under me, looking for that click. Then my mom calls me and says a friend of hers needs a receptionist because the girl in the job is going out on maternity leave. Would I do her a huge favor for three months?"

As she talked, she waved her hands, dipping and shaping the air, and he found himself smiling along with her as she recounted the story. Smiling and calculating exactly what it would take to get one of those hands on his body somewhere. He wasn't picky—not yet.

"Turns out Sheila, my mom's friend, runs an adoption agency. She's been a huge mentor to me and really helped me figure out what I wanted to do with my life. See, I love children, but I don't like teaching them. I do like helping them, though. I ended up staying at the agency for four years in various roles while I got my master's degree at night."

"You have a master's degree?" That revelation managed to get his attention off her mouth for a brief second. Not that he was shocked—she'd always been a great student. It was just one more layer to this woman that he didn't know nearly well enough.

"Yep." She nodded slowly. "The county requires it."

"That's great."

"What about you? I know you went into the military but that's about it. You went into the navy, Liam said."

"I did." He shifted uncomfortably, as he did any time his years in Afghanistan came up among civilians. The top secret nature of virtually every blessed op he'd completed was so ingrained, it was hard to have a regular conversation with anyone outside of his team. "Special operations. It's not as glamorous as the media makes it out to be. I sweated a lot, got really dirty and learned how to survive in just about any conditions. Meanwhile, I followed orders and occasionally gave a few. And now I'm home."

Something flashed deep in her eyes and she reached out. Her palm landed on his bare forearm, just below the rolled-up sleeve of his work shirt. "It doesn't sound glamorous. It sounds lonely."

"It was," he mumbled before he'd realized it. Shouldn't have admitted that. It smacked of weakness.

"I'm sorry." Her sympathy swept along his nerve endings, burying itself under his skin. The place she'd always been.

The place he'd always let her be. Because she soothed him and eased his loneliness. Always had. Looked as if for all the things that had changed, that was one constant, and he latched on to it greedily.

"It's over now."

His arm still stretched across the back of the seat. The slightest shift nestled her deeper against him and a strand of her glossy hair fell against her cheek. He wasted no time capturing it between his fingers, brushing it aside, and then letting his fingers linger.

Their gazes met and held for an eternity. A wealth of emotions swirled in her eyes.

Her skin was smooth and warm under his touch. She tilted her face toward his fingers, just a fraction of a movement. Just enough to tell him she wasn't about to push him away.

He slid his fingers more firmly under her chin and lifted it. And then those amazing lips of hers were within claiming distance. So he claimed them.

Grace opened beneath his mouth with a gasp, sucking him under instantly. Their mouths aligned, fitting together so perfectly, as if she'd been fashioned by the Almighty specifically for Kyle Wade. He'd always thought that. How was that still true?

The kiss deepened without any help on his part. He couldn't have said his own name as something raw and elemental exploded in his chest. *Grace.* The feel of her—like home and everything that was good in the world, blended together and infused into the essence of this woman.

He wanted more. And he couldn't have stopped himself from taking it.

Threading both hands through her hair, he cupped her head and changed the angle, plunging into the sensation. Taking her along with him. She moaned in her chest, and answering vibrations rocked his.

She clung to him, her hands gripping his shoulders as if she never wanted to let go. Which was great, because he didn't want her to.

Her sweet taste flowed across his tongue as he twined it with hers, greedily soaking up everything she was offering. It had been so long since he'd *felt*. Since he'd allowed himself to be so open. Hell, he hadn't *allowed* anything. She'd burrowed into his very core with nothing more than a kiss, and he'd had little to say about it.

And then she was gone. Ripped away.

She bolted from the rocker, her chest rising and falling as she hugged the split-pine railing surrounding the porch with her back. "I'm sorry. I shouldn't have done that."

"But you did." Ruthlessly, he shut down all the things she'd stirred up inside, since it appeared as if she wasn't up for seconds.

"I got caught up. That can't happen again."

Her expression glittered with undisguised longing, and no, he hadn't imagined that she'd welcomed his kiss. That she'd leaned into his touch and begged for more. So why was she stopping?

"I heartily disagree." He smiled, but it almost hurt to paint it on when his entire body was on fire. And this woman was the only one who could quench the flames. "It's practically a requirement for it to happen again."

"Are you that clueless, Kyle?"

Clueless. Yeah, he needed to catch a couple of clues apparently, like the big screaming back-off vibes Grace was shooting in his direction.

"I'm your daughters' caseworker," she reminded him with raised eyebrows. "We can't get involved."

His body cooled faster than if she'd dumped a bucket of ice water on his head. "You're right."

Of course she was right. When had he lost sight of that? This wasn't about whether she was interested or not; it was about his daughters. What had started out as a half-formed plan to distract her from work had actually distracted *him* far more effectively.

And he wanted to do it again. That was dangerous. She could take his girls away at the drop of a hat, and he couldn't afford to antagonize her. Hell, she'd even told him she had to treat the case as objectively as possible, and here he was, ignoring all of that.

Because she'd gotten to him. She'd dug under his skin without saying a word. Talk about dangerous. He couldn't let her know she had that much power over him, or she might use it to her advantage. How could he have forgotten how much better it was to keep his heart—and his mouth—shut? That's why he stuck to weekend hookups, like the one he'd had with Margaret. No one expected him to spill his guts, and then he was free to leave before anyone got a different idea about how things were going to go.

That was the best he could do. The best he *wanted* to do. But he couldn't ditch Royal this time around when things got too heated. He'd have to figure out how to get past one more tangle in the big fat knot in his chest that had Grace's name all over it.

She thought he was clueless? Just a big dumb guy who couldn't find his way around a woman without a map? Fine. It served his purpose to let her keep on thinking that, while he flipped this problem on its head.

"Sorry about that, then." He held up his hands and let a slow grin spread across his face. "Hands off from now on."

Or at least until he figured out which way the wind blew in Grace's mind about the custody issue. He couldn't afford to antagonize her, but neither could he afford to let her out of his sight. Once he had curried her good favor and secured his claim on his children, all bets were off.

And when she mumbled an excuse about having other dinner plans, he let her leave, already contemplating what kind of excuse he could find to get her into his arms again, but this time, without any of the emotional tangle she seemed to effortlessly cause.

Five

The kiss had been a mistake.

Grace knew that. She'd known *while* she was kissing Kyle. The whole time. Why, for the love of God, couldn't she stop thinking about it?

She'd kissed Kyle lots of times. None of those kisses was seared into her brain, ready to pop up in her consciousness like a jack-in-the-box gone really wrong. Of course, all her previous Kyle kisses had happened with the boy.

He was all man now.

Darker, harder, fiercer. And oh, how he had driven that fact home with nothing more than his mouth on hers. The feel of his lips had winnowed through her, sliding through her blood, waking it deliciously. Reminding her that she was all woman.

Telling her that she'd yet to fully explore what that meant.

Oh, sure, she'd kissed a few of the men she'd dated before she'd become a Professional Single Girl. But those chaste, dry pecks hadn't compared with being kissed by someone like Kyle.

She couldn't do it again. No matter how much she wanted to. No matter how little sleep she got that night and how little work she got done the next day because she couldn't erase the goose bumps from her skin that had sprung up the instant Kyle had touched her.

When Clare Connelly called with a dinner invitation, Grace jumped on it, nearly crying with relief at the thought of a distraction. Clare was a pediatric nurse who'd cared for the twin babies in the harrowing days after their premature birth, and she and Grace had become good friends.

Grace arrived at the Waters Café just off Royal's main street before Clare, so she took a seat at a four top and ordered a glass of wine while she waited. The café had been rebuilt as part of the revitalization of the downtown strip after the tornado had tried to wipe Royal off the map. The owners, Jim and Pam Waters, had nearly lost everything, but thanks to a good insurance policy and some neighborly folks, the café was going strong. Grace made it a point to eat there as often as possible, just to give good people her business.

Clare bustled through the door, her long blond hair still twisted up in her characteristic bun, likely because she'd just come from work at Royal Memorial. Grace waved, and then realized she wasn't alone—Clare had her arm looped through another woman's. Violet McCallum, who co-owned the Double M Ranch with her brother, Mac.

Wow, Grace hardly recognized her. Violet looked beautiful and was even wearing a dress instead of her usual boots and jeans. It had been a while since they'd seen each other. Not since they'd all met at Priceless, the antiques and craft store owned by Raina Patterson, to indulge in a girls' night of stained glass making, which had been so much fun that Grace had picked it up as a new hobby.

"I had to drag her out of the house," Clare said by way of greeting, laughing and pointing at Violet. It was a bit of a joke among the three ladies as Violet and Grace had done something similar for Clare when she'd been going through man troubles. "I hope you don't mind."

"Of course I don't. Hi, Violet!" Grace jumped up and embraced the auburn-haired woman. Violet gave her a one-armed hug in return and scuttled to a seat.

Grace and Clare settled into their own seats. Grace signaled the waitress, then leaned forward on her forearms to speak to Violet across the table. "What are you using on your skin? Because I'm investing in a truckload. You look positively luminous!"

Violet flinched and gave Grace a pained smile, which highlighted dark shadows in her friend's eyes. "Thanks. It's, um…my new apricot scrub. I'll text you the name of it when I get home."

"Sure," Grace said enthusiastically, but it felt a little forced. Something was off with Violet but she didn't want to pry. They'd been friends a long time. If Violet wanted to share what was up, she would. "Give me your hand, Clare. Dinner can't officially start until we ooh and aah over your ring!"

A smile split Clare's face, and she stuck her hand out, fingers spread in the classic pose of an engaged woman. "Stand back, ladies. This baby will blind you if you don't give it the proper distance."

Clare had recently gotten engaged to Dr. Parker Reese, a brilliant neonatal specialist at Royal Memorial, where they both worked. Their romance had been touch and go, framed by the desperate search for Maddie's mother after the infant had been abandoned at a truck stop shortly after her birth. Margaret Garner had then gotten into her car and given birth to Maggie a little farther down the road, ultimately dying from the traumatic childbirth. So the twins had ended up separated. When Maggie ultimately went home with Liam and Hadley, they were unaware she had a sister. Thankfully, they'd eventually realized Maddie and Maggie were twins and thus both belonged with the Wades.

Of course, that had all been before Kyle had come home.

And that was a dumb thing to start thinking about. Grace pinched herself under the table, but it didn't do any good. The kiss popped right back into her mind, exactly the thing she was trying to avoid thinking about.

Kyle was a difficult man to forget. She should know. She'd spent ten years trying to forget him and had failed spectacularly.

"Tell us about the wedding," Grace insisted brightly. Anything to take her attention off Kyle.

Clare gushed for a minute or two until the harried waitress finally made her way over to the three ladies. The ponytailed woman in her early twenties pulled a pen from behind her ear and held it expectantly over her order pad.

"Sorry for the wait, ladies," she apologized. "We're short-staffed today."

"No problem," Grace tossed out with a smile. "This Chardonnay is fabulous. Can you bring two more glasses?"

"No!" Violet burst out, and then her eyes widened as all three of the other women stared at her. "I, uh, didn't bring my driver's license, and I know you have to see my identification, so no drinking for me. Water is fine anyway. Thanks."

"It's okay, Ms. McCallum," the waitress said cheerfully. "I know you're over twenty-one. You were two years ahead of my sister in high school and she's twenty-four. I'd be happy to make an exception."

Violet turned absolutely green. "That's kind of you. But water is fine. Excuse me."

All at once, Violet rushed from the table, snatching her

purse from the back of the chair as she ran for the rear of the restaurant toward the bathrooms. In her haste, she knocked the straight-backed chair to the floor with a crash that reverberated in the half-full café. Conversations broke off instantly as the other customers swiveled to seek out the source of the noise.

Violet didn't pause until she'd disappeared from the room. *What in the world?*

"I practically had to force her to come tonight," Clare confessed, her voice lowered as she leaned close to Grace and waved off the beleaguered waitress, who promised to come back later. "I guess I shouldn't have. But she's been holed up for a few weeks now, and Mac called me, worried. He mentioned that she'd been under the weather, but he thought she was feeling better."

That was just like Violet's brother, Mac McCallum. He was the kind of guy Grace had always wished she'd had for a big brother, one who looked out for his sister even into their adulthood. Back in high school, he'd busted Tommy Masterson in the mouth for saying something off-color about Violet, and the boys in Royal had learned fast that they didn't cross Mac when it came to Violet.

"We should go check on her," Grace said firmly. Poor thing. She probably had a stomach flu or something like that, and they'd let her run off to the bathroom. Alone. "Friends hold each other's hair."

When Grace and Clare got to the restroom, Violet was standing at the sink, both hands clamped on the porcelain as she stared in the mirror, hollow eyed, supporting her full weight on her palms as if she might collapse if the vanity wasn't there to hold her up.

"You didn't have to disrupt your dinner on my account." Violet didn't glance at the other two women as she spoke into the mirror.

"Of course we did." Grace put her arm around Violet

and held her tight as she stood by her friend's side, offering the only kind of support she knew to give: physical contact. "Whatever it is, I'm sure you'll feel better soon. Sometimes it takes a while for the virus to work through your system. Do you want some crackers? Cold medicine? I'll run to the pharmacy if need be."

A brief lift of Violet's lips passed as a smile. "You're so nice to offer, but I don't think what I've got can be fixed with cold medicine."

She trembled under Grace's arm. This was no garden-variety stomach bug or spring cold, and Grace was just about to demand that Violet go see a doctor in the morning, or she'd drag her there herself, when Clare met Violet's eyes in the mirror as she came up on the other side of their friend.

"You're pregnant," Clare said decisively with a knowing smile. "I knew it. That night at Priceless... I could see then that you had that glowy look about you."

Oh. Now Grace felt like a dummy. Of course that explained Violet's strange behavior and refusal to drink the wine.

Shock flashed through Violet's expression but she banked it and then hesitated for only a moment. "No. That's impossible."

"Impossible, like you're in denial? Or impossible, like you haven't slept with anyone who could have gotten you pregnant?"

"Like, impossible, period, end of story, and now you need to drop it." Violet scowled at Clare in the mirror, who just stuck her tongue out. "It's just an upset stomach. Let's go back to the table."

With a nod that said she was dropping it but didn't like it, Clare hustled Violet to the table and ordered her hot tea with lemon, then ensured that everyone selected something to eat in her best mother-hen style.

The atmosphere grew lighter and lighter until their food came. They were just three friends having dinner, as advertised. Until Clare zeroed in on Grace and asked point-blank, "What's going on with you and Kyle Wade?"

Grace nearly choked. "What? Nothing."

Heat swept across her cheeks as she recalled in living color exactly how big a lie that was.

"Funny," Clare remarked to Grace. "I'd swear I heard mention of a highly charged *encounter* with Kyle in the parking lot of the HEB the other night. Care to fill us in?"

Violet perked up. "What's this? You're picking up with Kyle again?"

"Over my dead body!" That might have come out a little more vehement than she'd intended. "I mean…"

"I haven't seen him yet," Violet said to Clare as if Grace hadn't spoken. "But when I went to the bank yesterday, Cindy May said he's filled out and pretty much the stuff of centerfold fantasies. 'Smoking hot' was the phrase she used. Liberally."

Clare waggled her brows at Grace. "Spill the beans, dear."

Heat climbed up her cheeks. "I don't have any beans to spill. His daughters are on my case docket, and we ran into each other at the grocery store. This is Royal. It would be weird if I *hadn't* run into him."

"I haven't run into him." Violet sipped her tea. "Clare?"

The traitor shook her head. "Nope."

"Well, the Kyle train has left the station and I was not on board. I don't plan to be on board." Grace drained her glass of wine and motioned for another one the moment the waitress glanced her way. Wow, was it hot in here, and she was so thirsty. "Kyle Wade is the strong, silent type, and I need a man who can open his mouth occasionally to tell me what I mean to him. If that's not happening, I'm not happening. But it doesn't matter because nothing is going on with us. He's trying to be a father and I'm working to figure out how to let him. That's it."

All at once, she realized she'd already made up her mind about his fitness as a parent. Kyle was trying. She'd seen it over and over. What could she possibly object to in his bid for custody? Nothing. Any objections would be strictly due to hurt feelings over something that happened a decade ago. It was time to embrace the concept of bygones and move on.

"Men are nothing but trouble," Violet muttered darkly.

"That's not true," Clare corrected. "The right man is priceless."

"Parker is one in a million and he's taken. Unless you're willing to share?" Grace teased, and tried really hard to shut down the uncomfortable squeeze of jealousy surrounding her heart.

Clare had met her Dr. McDreamy. Grace had nothing. A great big void where Kyle used to be, and nothing had come along in ten years that could fill it. Well, except for the one man whom she suspected would fill that hole perfectly. She just had no desire to let him try, no matter how much she wanted a husband and family of her own.

Eyebrows raised, Clare cocked her head at Grace. "So you're sticking by your single-girl status, huh?"

She didn't sound so convinced, as if maybe Grace had been kidding when she'd vowed to be a Professional Single Girl from now on.

"I've been telling you so for months," Grace insisted. "There's nothing wrong with high standards and until I find someone who can spell *standards*, it's better to be on my own."

Actually, her standards weren't all that high—a run-of-the-mill swept-off-her-feet romance would do just fine. If she was pregnant and in love with a man who desperately loved her in return, she'd consider her life complete.

"Hear, hear." Violet raised her mug of hot tea to click it against Grace's wineglass. "I'll join your single girl club."

"Everyone is welcome. Except Clare." Grace grinned to cover the heaviness that had settled over her heart all at once. There wasn't anything on her horizon that looked like a fairy-tale romance. Just another meeting with a man who was driving her crazy.

Grace drove to Wade Ranch the next day without calling and without an appointment.

She didn't want to give Kyle any sort of heads-up that she was coming or that she'd made a decision. Hopefully, that meant she could get and keep the upper hand.

No more sunset conversations that ended with her wrapped up in Kyle's very strong, very capable arms.

No matter what. No matter how much she'd been arguing with herself that maybe Kyle had changed. Maybe *she* had changed. Maybe another kiss, exactly like that first one, would be what the doctor ordered, and then she would find out he'd morphed into her Prince Charming.

Yeah, none of that mattered.

Kyle and his daughters—that was what mattered. That morning she'd spent two hours in a room with her supervisor, Megan, going over her recommendation that Kyle be awarded full and uncontested custody of his children. With Megan's stamp of approval on the report, Grace's role in this long, drawn-out issue had come to a close.

Hadley answered the door at Wade House and asked after Grace's parents, then let Grace hold the babies without Grace having to beg too much. She inhaled their fresh powder scent—it was the best smell in the world. Out of nowhere, the prick of tears at her eyes warned her that she hadn't fully shut down the emotions from her conversation with Clare and Violet last night.

If this meeting went as intended, this might be her last

interaction with Kyle. And the babies. They were so precious and the thought of only seeing them again in passing shot through her heart.

"I'm here to see Kyle," she told Hadley as she passed the babies back reluctantly. She had a job to do, and it wasn't anyone's fault except hers that she didn't have a baby of her own.

"He's at the barn. Expect that will be the case from now on." Hadley shook her head in wonder. "I have to say, Kyle is nothing like I remember. He had no interest in the ranch before. Right? You remember that, too, don't you?"

Greedily, Grace latched on to the subject change and told herself it was strictly because she wanted additional validation that she was doing the right thing in trusting Kyle with his daughters. "I do recall that. But he's taking over the cattle side, or so I understand."

"That's right. Liam's about to come out of his skin, he's so excited about the prospect of focusing solely on his quarter horses. He didn't think Kyle was going to step up. But Liam has admitted to me, privately of course, that he might have been wrong about his brother."

Liam saw it, too. Kyle had changed.

That was very interesting food for thought.

"Do you think Kyle would mind if I visited him down at the barn? I need to talk to him about the report I'm filing."

Grace was already on her feet before she'd finished speaking, but Hadley just nodded with a smile. "Sure. Bring Kyle back with you and stay for lunch."

"Oh. Um…" Grace stared at Hadley gently rocking both babies in her arms and realized that her recommendations were going to affect Hadley and Liam, too. And not in a good way. She hated the fact that she was going to upset them after they'd spent so much love and effort in caring for Kyle's babies in his stead. There was a long conversation full of disappointment in Liam and Hadley's future.

All at once, she didn't want this job any longer. She should have figured out a way to pass the case off the moment she'd heard Kyle's name over the phone when Liam called. But she hadn't been able to, and people's lives were at stake here. She'd have to figure out how to handle it.

"Thanks for the lunch invite, but I have to be getting back to the office. Maybe next time," she said brightly, and escaped before Hadley could insist.

The cattle barn was a half mile down a chipped rock path to the west of Wade House, and faster than she would have liked, Grace pulled into the small clearing where a couple of other big trucks sat parked. She wandered into the barn, hoping Kyle would be inside.

He was.

The full force of his masculine beauty swept through her as she caught sight of him through the glass wall that partitioned the cattle office from the rest of the large barn. He was leaning against the frame of an open door, presumably talking to someone inside, hip cocked out in a way that should seem arrogant, but was just a testament to his incredible confidence.

Working man's jeans hugged his lean hips and yeah, he still had a prime butt that she didn't mind checking out in the slightest. There might be drool in her future.

And then Kyle backed out of the doorway and turned, catching her in the act of checking out his butt. *Shoot.* Too late, she spun around but not before witnessing the slow smile spreading across his face. How in the world was she going to brazen this out? Heat swirled through her cheeks.

Kyle exited the office area with a clatter. His eyes burned into her back and she had the distinct impression his gaze had dipped below her belt in a turnabout-is-fair-play-kind of checkout.

"Hey, Grace," he said pleasantly.

She couldn't very well ignore his greeting, so she sighed and faced him, smug smile and all. "Hi."

"See anything you like?"

How was she supposed to answer that? *Men*. They all had egos the size of Texas and she certainly wasn't going to cater to inflating his further. He was lucky she didn't smack him in his cocky mouth. "Nothing I haven't seen before."

Except she really shouldn't have been all high-and-mighty, when she was the one who'd been ogling his butt. It was her own darn fault she'd gotten caught.

"Really?" His eyebrows shot up and amusement played at his mouth. Not that she was staring at it or anything, or remembering how dark, hard and fierce that kiss had been. "You've been shopping for cattle before?"

"Cattle?" She made the mistake of meeting his glittery green eyes, vibrant even in the low light of the barn, and he sucked her in, mesmerizing her for a moment. "I…don't think… I'm not here to buy cattle."

Her fingers tingled all at once as they flexed in memory of clutching his shoulders the other night during their kiss. And then the rest of her body got in on that action, putting her somewhere in the vicinity of hot and bothered. A long liquid pull at her core distracted her entirely from whatever it was they were talking about.

"Are you sure? That's what we do here at Wade Ranch. Sell cattle. Figured you were in the market since you came all this way."

"Oh. No. No cattle." Geez, was there something wrong with her brain? Simple concepts like English and speaking didn't seem to be happening.

Kittens. Daffodils. She had to get her mind off that kiss with something that wasn't the slightest bit manly. But then Kyle shifted closer and she caught a whiff of something so wholly masculine and earthy and the slightest bit piney, it nearly made her weep with want.

"Well, then," he murmured. "Why are you here if it's not to peruse the goods?"

Oh, she was *so* here to peruse the goods. Except she wasn't and she couldn't keep falling down on the job. "I wanted to talk to you."

"Amazing coincidence. I wanted to talk to you, too."

"So I'm not bothering you?"

"Oh, yeah. Make no mistake, Grace. You bother me." His low, sexy voice skittered across her nerves, standing them on end. "At night, when I'm thinking about kissing you again. In the shower, when I'm *really* thinking about kissing you again. In the saddle, when I think kissing you again is the only thing that's going to make that particular position bearable."

A stupid rush of heat sprang up in her face as she pictured him riding a horse and caught his meaning.

It was uncomfortable for Kyle to sit in a saddle. Because he was turned on. By her.

It was embarrassing. And somehow empowering. The thrill of it sang through her veins. Being in love with Kyle she remembered. Being a source of discomfort, she didn't. Sex had been so new, so huge and so special the first time around. They hadn't really explored their physical relationship very thoroughly before everything had fallen apart due to Kyle's strange moods and inability to express his feelings for her.

She suddenly wondered what physical parts they'd left unexplored. And whether the superhot kiss—which had been vastly more affecting than the ones ten years ago— meant that he'd learned a few new tricks over the years.

"You've been thinking about our kiss, too?" she asked before she thought better of it.

"Too?" He picked up on that slip way too fast, his expression turning molten instantly as he zeroed in on her. "As in *also*? You've been thinking about it?"

He was aiming so much heat in her direction she thought she might melt from it.

"Um…" Well, it was too late to back out now. "Maybe once or twice. It was a nice kiss."

His slow smile set off warning bells. "*Nice.* I must be rusty if that's the best word you can come up with to describe it. Let me try again and I can guarantee *nice* won't be anywhere in your vocabulary afterward."

Before he could get started on that promise, she slapped a hand on his chest, and Lord have mercy, it was like concrete under her fingers, begging to be explored just to see if all of him was that hard.

"Not so fast," she muttered before she lost her mind completely. "I'm here in an official capacity."

"Well, why didn't you say so?"

"You were too busy trying to sell me a side of beef, if I recall," she responded primly, and his rich laugh nearly finished the job of melting her into a big puddle. She shouldn't let him affect her like that. Quickly, she snatched her hand back.

"Touché, Ms. Haines." He crossed his arms over his powerful chest and contemplated her, sobering slightly. "Is this about my girls?"

She nodded. "I've provided my recommendations in a report to my supervisor. But essentially, I have no objections to you having sole custody of your daughters."

Kyle let out a whoop and swept her up in his arms, spinning her around effortlessly. Laughing at his enthusiasm, she whacked him on the arm with token protests sputtering from her lips. This was not the appropriate way to thank his caseworker.

And then he let her slide to the floor again, much more

slowly than he should have, especially when it became clear that there was very little of him that wasn't hard.

She cleared her throat and stepped away.

"Thanks, Grace. This means a lot to me." Sincerity shone in his gaze and she couldn't look away. "So it's over? No more site visits?"

"Well…" She couldn't say it all at once. Her excuse to continue seeing him would evaporate if she said yes. "Maybe a few more. I still plan to keep an eye on you."

The vibe between them heated up again in a hurry as he leaned into her space. "But if you're not my daughters' caseworker any longer, then there's no reason I can't kiss you again."

True. But she couldn't have it both ways. Either she needed an excuse to keep coming by, even though that excuse would prevent anything from happening between them, or she could flat out admit she was still enormously attracted to him and let the chips fall where they may.

One option put butterflies in her stomach. And the other put caterpillars in it. The only problem was she couldn't figure out which was which.

"I'm not closing the case yet," she heard herself say before she'd fully planned to say it. "So I'll come by a couple more times, just to file additional support for the recommendation. It could still go the other way if anything changes."

"All right." He cocked his head. "But if you've already filed the report, there's no issue with your objectivity. Right?"

And maybe she should just call a spade a spade and settle things once and for all.

"Right. But—" she threw up a hand as a smile split his face "—that's not the only thing going on here, Kyle, and you know it. We haven't been a couple for a long time, and

I'm not sure picking up where we left off is the best idea. Not saying never. Just give me space for now."

So she could think. So she could figure out if she was willing to trust him again. So she could understand why everything between them felt so different this time, so much more dangerous and thrilling.

He nodded once, but the smile still plastered across his face said he wasn't convinced by her speech. Maybe because she hadn't convinced herself of it, either.

"You know where to find me. If you'll excuse me, I have some cattle to tend to."

She watched him walk off because she couldn't help herself apparently. And she had a feeling that was going to become a theme very shortly when interacting with Kyle Wade.

Six

Kyle didn't see Grace for a full week, and by the seventh day, he was starting to go a little bonkers. He couldn't stop thinking about her, about picking up that kiss again. Especially now that the conflict of interest had vanished.

But then she'd thrown up another wall—the dreaded *give me space*. He hated space. Unless he was the one creating it.

So instead of calling up Grace and asking her on a date the way he wanted to, he filled his days with things such as learning how to worm cattle alongside Doc Glade and his nights learning which of his daughters liked to be held a certain way.

It was fulfilling in a way he'd have never guessed.

And exhausting. Far more than going for days at a stretch with no sleep as he and his boys cleared a bayside warehouse of nasty snipers so American supply ships could dock without fear of being shot at.

Kyle would have sworn up and down that being a SEAL

had prepared him for any challenge, but he'd been able to perform that job with a sense of detachment. Oh, he'd cared, or he would never have put himself in the line of fire. But you had to march into a war knowing you might not come out. Knowing that you might cause someone else to not come out. There was no room for emotion in the middle of that.

Being a father? It was 100 percent raw emotion, 24-7. Fear that he was doing it wrong. Joy in simply holding another human being that was a part of him, who shared his DNA. Worry that he'd screw up his kids as his parents had done to him. A slight tickle in the back of his throat that it could all change tomorrow if Grace suddenly decided that she'd made a mistake in awarding him custody.

But above all else was the sense that he shouldn't be doing it by himself. Kids needed a mother. Hadley was nurturing and clearly cared about the babies, but she was Liam's wife, not Kyle's. Now that the news had come out about Grace's recommendations, it didn't seem fair to keep asking Hadley to be the nanny, not when she'd hoped to adopt the babies herself.

It was another tangle he didn't know how to unsnarl, so he left it alone until he could figure it out. Besides, no one was chomping at the bit to change the current living situation and for now, Kyle, Liam and Hadley shared Wade House with Maggie and Maddie. Which meant that it would be ridiculous to tell Hadley not to pick up one of his daughters when she cried. So he didn't.

Plus, he was deep in the middle of growing the cattle business. Calving season was upon them, which meant days and days of backbreaking work to make sure the babies survived, or the ranch lost money instantly. He couldn't spend ten or twelve hours a day at the cattle barn *and* take care of babies. That was his rationale anyway, and he repeated it to himself often. Some days it rang more true than others.

A week after Grace had told him he'd earned custody of his daughters, Kyle spent thirty horrific minutes in his office going through email and other stuff Ivy, Wade Ranch's bookkeeper and office manager, had dumped on his desk with way too cheery a smile. The woman was sadistic. Death by paper cuts might as well be Ivy's mantra.

God, he hated paperwork. He'd rather be hip-deep in manure than scanning vet reports and sales figures and bills and who knew what all.

A knock at his door saved him. He glanced up to see a smiling Emma Jane and he nearly wept in relief. Emma Jane had the best title in the whole world—sales manager—which meant he didn't have to talk to people who wanted to buy Wade Angus. She handled everything and he blessed her for it daily.

"Hey, boss," she drawled. "Got a minute?"

She always called him "boss" with a throaty undertone that made him vaguely uncomfortable, as if any second now, she might declare a preference for being dominated and fall at his feet, prostrate.

"For you, always." He kicked back from the desk and crossed his arms as the sales manager came into his office. "What's up?"

With a toss of her long blond hair, Emma Jane sashayed over to his desk and perched one hip on the edge, careful to arrange her short skirt so it revealed plenty of leg. Kyle hid a grin, mostly because he didn't want to encourage her. God love her, but Emma Jane had the subtlety of a Black Hawk helicopter coming in for landing.

"I was thinking," she murmured with a coy smile. "We've mostly been selling cattle here locally, but we should look to expand. There's a big market in Fort Worth."

Obviously she was going somewhere with this, so Kyle

just nodded and made a noncommittal sound as he waited for the punch line.

"Wade Ranch needs to make some contacts there," she continued, and rearranged her hair with a practiced twirl. "We should go together. Like a business trip, but stay overnight and take in the sights. Maybe hit a bar in Sundance Square?"

First half of that? Great plan. Spot-on. Second half was so not a good idea, Kyle couldn't even begin to count the ways it wasn't a good idea. But he had to tread carefully. Wade Ranch couldn't afford for Kyle to antagonize another employee into quitting. Liam still hadn't replaced Danny Spencer, and Kyle was starting to worry his brother was going to announce that he'd decided *Kyle* should be the ranch manager.

"I like the way you think," he allowed. "You're clearly the brains of this operation."

She batted her lashes with a practiced laugh, leaning forward to increase the gap at her cleavage. "You're such a flatterer. Go on."

Since it didn't feel appropriate for the boss to be staring down the front of his employee's blouse, no matter how obvious she was making it that she expected him to, Kyle glanced over Emma Jane's shoulder to the window. And spied the exact person he'd been hoping to see. *Grace*. Finally.

He'd been starting to wonder if she was planning to avoid him for the next ten years. From the corner of his eye, he watched her park her green Toyota in the small clearing outside the barn and walk the short path to the door. His peripheral vision was sharp enough to see a sniper in a bell tower at the edge of a village—or one social worker with hair the color of summer wheat at sunset, who had recently asked Kyle to give her space.

"No, really," he insisted as he focused on Emma Jane

again. Grace had just entered the barn, judging by the sound of the footsteps coming toward his office, which he easily recognized as hers. "You've been handling cattle sales for what, almost a year now? Your numbers are impressive. Clearly you know your stuff."

Or she knew how to stick her breasts in a prospective buyer's face. Honestly, there was no law against it, and he didn't care how she sold cattle as long as she did her job. Just as there was no law against letting Grace think there was more going on here in his office than there actually was.

She wanted space, didn't she? Couldn't give a woman any more space than to pretend he'd moved on to another one. If he timed it right, Grace would get an eyeful of exactly how much *space* he was giving her. He treated Emma Jane to a wide smile and put an elbow on the desk, right by her knee.

Emma Jane lit up, just as Grace appeared in the open doorway of his office.

"Thanks, sweetie." Emma Jane smiled and ran one hand up his arm provocatively. He didn't remove it. "That's the nicest compliment anyone's ever given me."

Grace halted as if she'd been slapped. That's when he turned his head to meet her gaze, acknowledging her presence, just in case she'd gotten it into her head to flee. She was right where he wanted her.

"Am I interrupting?" Grace asked drily, and Emma Jane jerked back guiltily as she figured out they weren't alone anymore.

Yes, thank God. He'd have to deal with Emma Jane at some point, but he couldn't lie—he'd much rather have Grace sitting on his desk and leaning over strategically any day of the week and twice on Sunday.

"Not at all." Kyle stood with a dismissive nod at Emma Jane, whose usefulness had just come to an end. "We were just talking about how to increase our contact list in the Fort Worth area. We can pick it up later."

"We sure can," Emma Jane purred, and then shot Grace a dirty look as she flounced from the room.

"That was cozy," Grace commented once the sales manager was out of earshot. Her face was blank, but her tone had an undercurrent in it that he found very interesting.

"You think so?" Kyle crossed his arms and cocked a hip, pretending to contemplate. "We were just talking. I'm not sure what you mean."

Grace rolled her eyes. "Really, Kyle? She was practically draped over your desk like a bearskin throw rug, begging you to wrap her around you."

Yeah. She pretty much had been. He bit back a grin at Grace's colorful description. "I didn't notice."

"Of course you didn't." Her eyebrows snapped together over brown eyes that—dare he hope—had a hint of jealousy glittering in them. "You were too busy being blinded by her cleavage."

That got a laugh out of him, which didn't sit well with Grace, judging by the fierce scowl on her face. But he couldn't help it. This was too much fun. "She is a nice-looking woman, I do agree."

"I didn't say that. She's far too obvious to be considered 'nice-looking.'" Grace accompanied this with little squiggly motions of her forefingers. "She might as well write her phone number on her forehead with eyeliner. She clearly buys it in bulk and layers it on even at ten o'clock in the morning, so what's a little more?"

The more Grace talked, the more agitated she became, drawing in the air with her whole hand instead of just her fingers.

"So she's a little heavy-handed with her makeup." He waved it off. "She's a great girl who sells cattle for Wade Ranch. I have no complaints with her."

Grace made a little noise of disgust. "Except for the way she was shamelessly flirting with you, you mean? I can't believe you let her talk to you like that."

"Like what?" He shrugged, well aware he was pouring gasoline on Grace's fire, but so very curious what would happen when she exploded. "We were just talking."

"Yeah, you're still just as clueless as you always were."

There was that word again. *Clueless*. She'd thrown it at him one too many times to let it go. There was something more here to understand. He could sense it.

Before he could demand an explanation, Johnny blew into the office, his chest heaving and mud caked on his jeans and boots from the knee down. "Kyle. We got a problem. One of the pregnant cows is stuck in the ravine at the creek and she went into labor."

Instantly, Kyle shouldered past a wide-eyed Grace with an apologetic glance. He hated to leave her behind but this was his job.

"Take me there."

Liam had put Kyle in charge of the cattle side of Wade Ranch. This was his first real test and the gravity of it settled across his shoulders with weight he wasn't expecting.

He followed Johnny to the paddock where they kept their horses and mounted up, ignoring the twinge deep in his leg bone, or what was left of it. He could sit in his office like a wimp and complain about paperwork or ride. There was no room for a busted leg in ranching.

Kyle heeled Lightning Rod into a gallop and tore after Johnny as the ranch hand led him across the pasture where the pregnant herd had been quartered—to prevent the very problem Johnny had described. The expectant cows shouldn't have been anywhere near the creek that ran along the north side of Wade Ranch.

Kyle hadn't been there in years but he remembered it. He and Liam had played there as boys, splashing through the shallow water and gigging for frogs at dusk as the fat reptiles croaked out their location to the two bloodthirsty boys. Calvin had made them clean and dress the frogs when he found out, and they had frog legs for dinner that night. It was a lesson Kyle never forgot—eat what you kill.

They arrived at the edge of the pasture in a couple of minutes. A fence was down. That explained it.

"What happened?" Kyle asked as he swung out of the saddle to inspect the downed barbed wire and wooden stake.

"Not sure. Slim and I were running the fence and found this. Then he went to the creek to check it out. Sure 'nuff, one of the cows had wandered off. Still don't know how she got down there. Slim stayed with her while I came and got you."

"Good man. Hustle back to the barn and grab some of the guys to get this repaired," Kyle instructed, his mind already blurring with a plan. He just had to check out the situation to make sure the extraction process currently mapping itself out in his head was viable.

Johnny nodded and galloped off.

Kyle let Lightning Rod pick his way along the line of the creek until he saw Slim down in the ravine, hovering over the cow. She was still standing, which was good. As soon as a cow lay down, that meant they had less than an hour until she'd start delivering. They'd have to work fast or she'd be having her baby on that thin strip of ground between the steeply sloped walls and the creek. If the calf was in the wrong position, it would be too hard to assist with the birth, and besides, all the equipment was back at the barn.

Somehow, he had to figure out how to get her out. Immediately. Clearly, Slim had no idea how to do it or he wouldn't have sent Johnny after the boss. This was Kyle's battle to lose. So he wouldn't lose.

Kyle galloped another hundred feet to check out the slope of the creek bed walls, but they were just as steep all the way down the culvert as they were at the site where the cow had gone down. As steep as they'd been when he was a boy. He and Liam had slid down the slope on their butts, ruining more than one pair of pants in the process because it was too steep to walk down. But that had been in August when it was dry. In March, after a cold winter and wet spring, the slope was nothing but mud. Which probably explained how the cow had ended up at the bottom—she'd slipped.

Kyle planned to use that slick consistency to his advantage.

"Slim," he called down. "You okay for another few minutes? I have to run back to the barn to get a couple of things, and then we're gonna haul her out."

Slim eyed Kyle and then the cow. "*Haul* her out? That's a dumb idea. And not what Danny Spencer would have done."

Too bad. Wade Ranch was stuck with Kyle, not the former ranch manager. "Yep."

Not much else to say. It wasn't as if he planned to blubber all over Slim and ask for a chance to prove he could be as good as Spencer. He firmed his mouth and kept the rest inside. Like always.

The ranch hand nodded, but his expression had that I'll-believe-it-when-I-see-it vibe.

Kyle galloped back to the barn and found exactly what he was looking for—the pair of hundred-foot fire hoses Calvin had always kept on hand in case of emergency. They'd been retrofitted with a mechanism that screwed into the water reservoir standing next to the barn. The stock was too valuable to wait on the city fire brigade in the event of a barn fire, so a smart rancher developed his own firefighting strategy.

Today, the hoses were going to lift a cow out of a creek bed.

Kyle jumped into the Wade Ranch Chevy parked near the barn and drove across the pasture, dodging cows and the stretches of grass that served as their grazing ground as best he could. Fortunately, Johnny and the other hands hadn't fixed the fence yet, so Kyle drove right through the break to the edge of the creek.

By the time he skidded to a halt, the hands had gathered around to watch the show. There was no time to have a conversation about this idea, nor did Kyle need anyone else's approval, so if they didn't like it, they could keep it to themselves. Grimly, Kyle pulled the hoses from the truck bed and motioned to Johnny.

"I'm going to tie these to the trailer hitch and then throw them down to Slim. I'll rappel down and back up again once we have the hoses secured around the cow. You drive while I watch the operation. We'll haul her out with good old-fashioned brute strength."

Johnny and the other hands looked dubious but Kyle ignored them and got to work on tying the hoses, looping one end around the trailer hitch into a figure-eight follow-through knot. It was the best knot to avoid slipping and his go-to, but he'd never used it on a fire hose. Hopefully it would hold, especially given that he was the one who would be doing the rappelling without a safety harness.

When the hoses were as secure as a former SEAL could get them, Kyle tossed the ends down to Slim and repeated the plan. Slim, thankfully, just nodded and didn't bother to express his opinion about the chances of success, likely because he figured it was obvious.

Kyle waited for Slim to drop the hoses, and then grabbed on to one. His work gloves gripped better than he was expecting, a plus, given the width of the line. Definitely not the kind of rappelling he was used to, but he probably had more experience at this kind of rescue than anyone there.

He'd lost count of the number of times he'd led an extraction in hostile conditions with few materials at his disposal. And usually he was doing it with a loaded pack and weapons strapped to his back. Going down into a ravine after a cow was a piece of cake in comparison.

Until his boot slipped.

His bad leg slammed into the ground and he bit back a curse as a white-hot blade of pain arced through his leg. *Idiot*. He should have counterbalanced differently to compensate for his cowboy boots, which were great for riding, but not so much for slick mud.

Sweat streamed down his back and beaded up on his forehead, instantly draining down into his eyes, blinding him. Now his hell was complete. And he was only halfway down.

Muttering the lyrics to a Taylor Swift song that had always been his battle cry, he focused on the words instead of the pain. The happy tune reminded him there was still good in the world, reminded him of the innocent teenagers sitting at home in their bright, colorful rooms listening to the same song. They depended on men like Kyle to keep them safe. He'd vowed with his very life that he would. And he'd carried that promise into the darkest places on the planet while singing that song.

Finally, he reached the bottom and took a quarter of a second to catch his breath as he surveyed the area. Cow still standing. Hoses still holding. He nodded to Slim and they got to work leading the cow as close to the slope as possible, which wasn't easy, considering she was in labor, scared and had the brain of a—well, a cow.

The next few minutes blurred as Kyle worked alongside Slim, but eventually they got the makeshift harness in place. Kyle hefted the heavy hoses over his shoulder and climbed back up the way he'd come. The men had shuffled to the edge of the ravine to watch, backing up the closer Kyle got to the top. He hit the dirt at the edge and rolled onto the hoses to keep them from sliding back to the bottom.

He was not making that climb again.

Johnny grabbed hold of the hoses so Kyle could stand, and then made short work of tying them to the trailer hitch next to the other ends. He waved at Johnny to get in the truck. It was do-or-die time.

Johnny gunned the engine.

"Slow," Kyle barked.

The truck inched forward, pulling up all the slack in the hoses. And then the tires bit into the ground as the truck strained against the load. The cow balked but the hoses held her in place. So far so good.

The hoses gradually pulled the cow onto her side and inched her up the slope as the truck revved forward a bit more. It was working. The mud helped her slide, though she mooed something fierce the whole time.

Miraculously, after ten nail-biting minutes, the cow stood on solid ground at the top of the ravine. Kyle's arms ached and his gloves had rubbed raw places on his fingers, but it was done.

Johnny jumped from the truck and rushed over to clap him on the back, breaking the invisible barrier around Kyle. The other ranch hands swarmed around as well, smiling and giving their own version of a verbal high-five. Even Slim offered a somewhat solemn, "Good job."

Kyle took it all with good humor and few words because what was he supposed to say? *Told you so? That's okay, boys. I'm the boss for a reason?*

The ranch hands wandered off, presumably to finish the job of fixing the fence. Eventually, Kyle stood there, alone. Which was par for the course.

Was it so bad to have hoped this would become his new team?

No. The bad part was that if a successful bovine extraction couldn't solidify his place, he suspected nothing would. Because everyone was still waiting around for him to either fail or leave. Except Kyle.

Even Grace didn't fully believe in him yet, or she wouldn't have qualified her recommendations with a "We'll see," and the threat that she wasn't closing the case.

What more did he have to do to prove that honor, integrity and loyalty were in his very fiber?

Grace stood at the wide double door of the barn and watched horses spill into the yard as the hands returned from the cow emergency. They dismounted and loudly recounted the rescue with their own versions of the story. Seems as if Kyle had used fire hoses to drag the animal out of the ravine, which the hands alternately thought was ingenious or crazy depending on who was doing the talking.

Apparently it had worked, since one of the ranch hands had the cow in question on a short lead.

She should have left. She'd told Kyle what she'd come to say, witnessed an exchange between Kyle and another woman that she hadn't been meant to see, and now she was done. But you could have cut the tension in the barn with a chain saw, and she'd been a little bit worried about Kyle. Sure, he'd grown up on the ranch, but that didn't automatically make him accident-proof.

No one mentioned anything about Kyle, so he must be okay. But she wanted to see him for herself. Once she'd assured herself of it—strictly in her capacity as his daughters' caseworker, of course, no other reason—then she'd leave.

Finally, the truck he'd taken off in rolled into the yard and he swung out of the cab, muddy and looking so worn, she almost flew to his side. Except the little blonde bearskin rug beat her to it. Emma Jane. Or as Grace privately liked to call her—The Tart.

Like a hummingbird auditioning for the part of the town harlot, Emma Jane fluttered over to Kyle, expertly sashaying across the uneven ground in her high-heeled boots, which drew the attention of nearly every male still milling around the yard, except the one she was after.

Kyle pulled long lines of flat, muddy hoses out of the bed of the truck, dragged them to the spigot on the water tower beside the barn and attached one, using it to hose off the other.

Which was also pretty ingenious in her opinion.

Emma Jane crowded Kyle at the water tower, smiling and gesturing. Grace was too far away to hear what she was saying, but she probably didn't need to hear it to know it was along the lines of *Oh, Kyle, you're a hero* or the even more inane *Oh, Kyle, you're so strong and brave!*

Please. Well, yes, he was all of those things, no question, but Grace didn't see the point in shoving half-exposed breasts in a man's face when you said them.

The strong and brave hero in question glanced up at Emma Jane as he performed his task. And smiled. It was his slow, slightly naughty smile that he'd flashed Grace right after kissing her senseless, the one that had nearly enticed her back into his arms because it was so sexy.

It was a smile that told a woman he liked what he saw, that he had a few thoughts about what he planned to do with her. And there he was, aiming it at another woman!

That…*dog.*

Breathe, Grace. He was just smiling.

She crossed her arms, leaning forward involuntarily though there was no way she would be able to pick up the conversation from this distance, not with the clatter going on in the yard, all the hands still chattering and watering their horses at the trough running between the water tower and the barn.

Then Emma Jane placed her talons on Kyle's arm and he leaned into it. Something hot bloomed in Grace's chest as she imagined him kissing Emma Jane the way he'd kissed her. He said something to Emma Jane over his shoulder and she laughed. Grace didn't have to hear what was being said. He was enjoying Emma Jane's attention, obviously.

Or he was just washing a hose and having a conversation with his employee, which was none of her business, she reminded herself. She didn't own Kyle, and he'd certainly had female companions over the years who weren't Grace, or he wouldn't currently have two daughters.

She'd just never had that shoved in her face so blatantly before.

Now would be a great time to leave. Except as she started back to her car, Kyle stood and walked straight toward her, calling to one of the hands to lay the hoses out to dry before putting them away. Emma Jane trailed him, still chattering.

He was coming to talk to Grace. With Emma Jane in tow.

Or Kyle could be walking toward the barn. Grace *was* standing in the doorway.

But then his gaze met hers and the rest of the activity in the yard fell away as something wholly encompassing washed through her.

Seven

"Ms. Haines." Kyle nodded.

And then walked right past her!

Had she just been dismissed? Grace scowled and pivoted to view the interior of the barn. Kyle squeezed Emma Jane's shoulder at the door of the office and The Tart disappeared beyond the glass, presumably to go sharpen her claws.

Then he strolled across the wide center of the barn and disappeared around a corner.

Without a single ounce of forethought, Grace charged after him. She'd waited around, half-crazy with worry to assure herself he was okay, and he couldn't bother to stop and talk to her? How dare he? Emma Jane had certainly gotten more than a perfunctory nod and a platitude.

She skidded around the corner, an admonishment already forming in her mouth.

It vanished as she rounded the corner into a small, enclosed area. Kyle stood at a long washbasin. *Wet. Shirtless. Oh, my.*

Obviously she should have thought this through a little better.

Speechless, she stared unashamedly at his bare, rippling torso as he dumped another cupful of water down it. Water streamed along the cut muscles, running in rivulets through the channels to disappear into the fabric of his jeans.

Some of it splashed on her. She was too close. And way too far.

Every ounce of saliva fled from her mouth, and she couldn't have torn her gaze from his gorgeous body for a million dollars. She'd have *paid* a million dollars, if she'd had it, to stand in this spot for an eternity.

"Something else you wanted, Ms. Haines?"

She blinked and glanced up into his diamond-hard green eyes, which were currently fastened on her as he glanced over his shoulder. Busted. Again. There was no way to spin this into anything other than it was. "I didn't know you were washing up. Sorry."

Casually, he turned and leaned back against the long sink, arms at his side, which left that delicious panorama of naked chest right there on display. "That really didn't answer my question, now, did it?"

He was turning her brain mushy again, because she surely would have remembered if there had been talking. "Did you ask me a question?"

His soft laugh crawled under her skin. "Well, I'm trying to figure out what it is that you're after, Grace. Maybe I should ask a different way. Are you here to watch, or join in? Because either is fine with me."

Her ire rushed back all at once, melding uncomfortably with the heat curling through her midsection at the suggestion. "That's a fine way to talk after flirting with Ms. Cattle Queen."

Kyle just raised an eyebrow. "Careful, or a man might start to think you cared whether he flirted with another woman. That's not the case. Right?"

She crossed her arms, but those diamond-hard eyes drilled through her anyway. "Oh, you're right. I don't care." Loftily, she waved off his question. "It just seems disingenuous to make time with one woman mere minutes before inviting another one to *wash up.*"

All at once, she had a very clear image of him dumping a cup of water over her chest and licking it off. The heat in her core snaked outward, engulfing her whole body. And that just made her even madder. Kyle was a big flirt who could get Grace hot with merely a glance. It wasn't fair.

She didn't remember him affecting her that way before. And she would have. This was all new and exciting and frustrating and scary.

"Maybe." That slow smile spilled onto his face. "But you're the one standing here. I'm not offering to *wash up* with Emma Jane."

"Yeah. Only because she didn't have the foresight to follow you."

"You did." He watched her without blinking and spread his arms. "Here I am. Whatever are you going to do with me?"

That tripped off a whole chain reaction inside as she thought long and hard about the answer to that question. But she hadn't followed him for *that.* Not that she knew for sure he even meant *that.* But regardless, he had a lot of nerve.

Hands firmly on her hips—just in case they developed a mind of their own and started wandering along the ridges and valleys of that twelve-pack of abs, which she was ashamed to admit she'd counted four times—she glared at him. "This is not you, Kyle. Liam? Yeah. He's a playboy and a half, but you've never been like that, just looking for the next notch in your bedpost."

There. That was the point she was trying to make.

He laughed with genuine mirth. "Is that what you think this is? Kyle Wade, playboy in training. It has a nice ring. But that ain't what's going on."

"Then by all means. Tell me what's going on," she allowed primly.

"Emma Jane is my employee. That's it." He sliced the air with his hand. "You, on the other hand, are something else."

"Oh, yeah? What?"

He swept her with a once-over that should not have been so affecting, but goodness, even the bottoms of her feet heated up. "A woman I'd like to kiss. A lot."

As in he wanted to kiss her several times or he just wanted to really badly?

She shook her head. Didn't matter.

"Well, be that as it may." She tossed her head, scrambling to come up with a response, and poked him in the chest for emphasis. He glanced down at her finger and back up at her, his eyelids shuttered slightly. "You wanted to kiss Emma Jane a minute ago. Pardon me for not getting in line."

"Grace." Her name came out so garbled, she hardly recognized it. "I do not want to kiss Emma Jane."

"Could have fooled me. And her. She definitely had the impression you were into her. Maybe because you were telling her jokes and letting her put her hands all over you."

"And maybe I let her because I knew you were watching."

"I— What?" All the air vanished from her lungs instantly. And then she found it again. "It was on purpose? Flirting with Emma Jane. You did that on *purpose*?" She was screeching. Dang near high enough to call dogs from another county. "Oh, that's…"

She couldn't think of a filthy enough word to describe it. *He'd been playing her.* Kyle Wade had picked her up and played her like a violin. Of course he had. She might as well have Bad Judge of Character tattooed on her forehead so people could get busy right away with pulling one over on her. And she'd waltzed to his tune with nary a peep.

And speaking of no peeps, Kyle was standing there watching her without saying a word, the big jerk.

"It was all a lie?" she asked rhetorically, because he'd just said it was, though why he'd done it, she couldn't fathom. "What were you trying to accomplish, anyway?"

His grin slipped as he pinned her in place with nothing more than his gaze. He swayed forward, just a bit, but his heat reached out and slid along her skin as if he'd actually brushed her torso with his.

She couldn't move. Didn't want to move. The play of expression across his face fascinated her. The heat called to her.

"No lies. See this," he murmured and wagged a finger between them, drawing her eye as he nearly touched her but didn't. "Just what you ordered. Space. Anytime you feel inclined to make it disappear, I'll be the one over here minding my own business."

Oh! Of all the sneaky, underhanded, completely accurate things to say.

Mute, she stared at him and he stared right back. He'd been giving her exactly what she asked for. Never mind that she'd rather drink paint thinner than admit he might have a point. And the solution was rather well spelled out, too.

She didn't want him to flirt with other women? Then close the gap.

There was no more running, no more hiding. This was it, right here. He wanted her. But he wasn't going to act on it.

They shared a fierce attraction and the past was in the past. She'd held him at bay in order to get her feet under her, to make sure he wasn't going to hurt her again. It was the same tactic she employed with her cases. If she wanted to be sure she wasn't letting her emotions get the best of her, wanted to be sure she was making an unbiased decision, she stepped back. Assessed from afar with impersonal attention.

This wasn't one of her cases. This was Kyle. As personal as it got. And the only way she could fully assess what they could have now was to dive into that pool. Wading in an inch at a time wasn't working.

Rock solid, not moving a muscle, he watched her. This was her show and he was subtly telling her he'd let her run it. Except he was also saying she couldn't keep talking out of both sides of her mouth.

Either she could act like a full-grown woman and do something about the man she wanted or keep letting their interaction devolve into an amateurish high school game.

She picked doing something.

Going on instinct alone, she reached out with both hands and pressed them to Kyle's bare chest, her gaze on his as she did it, gauging his reaction. His eyes darkened as her fingers spread and she flattened both palms across his pectoral muscles. Damp. Hot. Hard.

One muscle flexed under her touch and she almost yanked her hands back. But she didn't. He hadn't felt like this before. He was all man and it was a serious turn-on, especially because it was still Kyle underneath. When he was looking at her the way he was right then, as if the center of the universe had been deposited in his palm, it was easy to remember why she'd fallen for him. All the emotion of being in love with this man rushed back.

"There you go," she said breathlessly. "No more space."

"Grace," he growled, and she felt the vibrations under her fingers. "You better mean it. I'm only human."

Her touch was affecting him. *She* was affecting *him*. It was something she hadn't fully contemplated, but she did get that it wasn't fair to lead him on and keep dancing back and forth between yes and no.

"I mean it. If you want to kiss me, it's fine."

"*Fine*." There came that slow smile. "That's almost as bad a word as *nice*. I think it's time to fix your vocabulary."

All at once, Kyle's arms snaked around her, yanking her tight against his hard body. But before she could fully register the contact, his mouth claimed hers.

The crash of lips startled her. And then she couldn't think at all as his hands slid down her back, touching her, trailing heat along her spine, sliding oh, so slowly against her bottom to finally grip her hips and hold them firmly, pulling her taut against his body.

His very aroused body. The length of him pressed into her soft flesh as he kissed her. It was a whole-body experience, and nothing like the front porch kiss that she'd thought was so memorable that she couldn't shake it. That kiss had been wonderful, but tame.

This was a grown-up kiss.

The difference was unfathomable.

This kiss was hungry, questing, begging for more even as he took it.

Kyle changed the angle, diving deeper into her mouth, thrilling her with the intensity. His tongue swirled out, and instinctively, she met him with her own. He groaned and she felt it to her toes.

Kyle. She'd missed the feel of him in her arms. Missed the scent of him in her nose.

Except this Kyle wasn't like the warm coat she'd envisioned sliding into, wholly familiar and so comforting.

No, this Kyle was like opening a book expecting a nice story with an interesting plot and instead falling into an immersive world full of dark secrets and darker passions.

His hands were everywhere, along her sides, thumbs circling and sliding higher until he found her breasts beneath her clothes. The contact shot through her as he touched her, and then he shoved a leg between hers, tilting his hips to rub against her intimately.

This was not a kiss—it was a seduction.

And she had just enough functioning brain cells to be aware that they were not only in a barn, but she hadn't fully figured out what was supposed to come next. She didn't know what had changed that might mean things would work between them this time. She didn't fully trust that he was here for good, and even if he was, that he was going to meet her standards any better today than he had ten years ago.

Oh, he was certainly earning a ten in the Sweeping Her Off Her Feet category. But Happily Ever After carried just as much weight as Expressing His Feelings. And neither of those were on the board yet.

Breaking off the kiss—and nearly kicking herself at the same time—she pushed back and mumbled, "Wait."

His torso shuddered as he dragged in a ragged breath. "Because?"

"You know why." Her Professional Single Girl status was in jeopardy and she had to make sure he was worth the price of relinquishing it. Sure, he was hot and a really great kisser, but she didn't sleep around. An interlude in the barn didn't change that.

"I did not develop ESP at any point in the last ten years," he rasped, his expression going blank as he stared at her.

"Because of what happened before, Kyle." Exasperated, she stared at the wall over his head so his delicious chest wasn't right in her field of vision. "There's a lot of leftover emotion and scrambled-up stuff to sort out. I have to take it slow this time."

"Then you should leave," he said curtly. "Because I'm definitely not in the mood for slow right now."

She took his advice and fled. It wasn't until she'd reached her car and slid into the driver's seat that she realized leaving was the one surefire way to *never* figure out what they could have together.

Maybe slow wasn't any better an idea than space.

And at this moment, the only *s* word she seemed capable of thinking about ended in *ex*, which was the crux of the problem. She and Kyle had a former relationship and it muddied everything, especially her feelings.

Kyle stabbed his hands through his shirt, nearly ripping the sleeve off in the process.

Grace wanted to take it *slow* because of what had happened before.

Furiously, he fingered the buttons through the holes haphazardly, none too happy about having to spend the rest of the workday with a hard-on he couldn't get rid of, no matter what he thought of to kill his arousal—slugs, the Cowboys losing the Super Bowl, his mother. Nothing worked because the feel of Grace in his arms was way too fresh, and had been cut way too short.

Because of what had happened *before*. She meant when she'd fallen for Liam and he'd thrown her over. While Kyle appreciated that she wanted to figure out her own mind before taking things further with him, he wasn't about to stand by and let what happened in the past with his brother ruin the present.

Liam was married now and Grace should be completely over all of that. Bygones included forgetting about *everything* that happened in the past.

He didn't have any choice but to let it go for the time being. He had a job to do and men to manage.

By the time the sun set, the entire Wade Ranch staff was giving Kyle a wide berth. So the cow extraction hadn't earned him any points. Figured. His surly mood didn't help and he finally just called it a day.

When he got back to the main house, Liam met him in the mudroom off the back.

"Hey," Liam called as Kyle sat on the long bench seat to remove his boots, which were a far sight cleaner than they'd been earlier, but still weren't fit to walk the floors inside.

Kyle jerked his chin, not trusting himself to actually speak to anyone civilly. Though if anyone deserved the brunt of his temper, it was Liam.

"Hadley and I are flying to Vail this weekend. Just wanted to give you a heads-up." Liam's mouth tightened. "You'll be okay handling the babies for a couple of days by yourself, right?"

"Yep."

Liam hesitated, clearly expecting more of a conversation or maybe even an argument about it, but what else was there to say? Kyle couldn't force the couple to stay, and Maddie and Maggie were his kids. He'd figure it out. Somehow. The little pang in his stomach must be left over from Grace. Probably.

"Okay. We're leaving in an hour or so."

Kyle let the first boot hit the floor with a resounding *thunk* and nodded. Liam kept talking.

"I'm flying my Cessna, so it's no problem to delay for a bit if you need to talk to Hadley about anything."

The other boot hit the floor. Hadley had already imparted as much baby knowledge as she possibly could. Another hour of blathering wasn't going to make a difference. "Not necessary."

Liam still didn't leave. "You have my cell phone number. It's okay if you want to call and ask questions."

"Yep."

Geez. Was his brother really that much of an ass? Liam had taken care of the babies before Kyle had gotten there without anyone standing over him waiting for his first mistake. Did Liam really think babysitting was something only he could do and that Kyle was hopelessly inept? Seemed so. Which only set Kyle's resolve.

He wouldn't call. Obviously Liam and Hadley had plans that didn't include taking care of Kyle's children. Who was he to stand in the way of that? Never mind that Kyle had never even stayed alone in the house with the babies. Hadley had always just been there, ready to pick up the slack.

This was the part where Kyle wished he had someone like Hadley. His kids needed a mother. Problem was, he could only picture Grace's face when thinking of a likely candidate. And she was too skittish about *everything*. Mentioning motherhood would likely send her over the edge.

Finally, Liam shuffled off to finish packing or whatever, leaving Kyle to his morose thoughts. It was fine, really. So he'd envisioned asking Grace if she'd like to drive into Odessa for dinner and a movie. Get out of Royal, where there were no prying eyes. Maybe he would have even talked her into spending the night in a swanky motel. He had scads of money he never spent and he couldn't think of anyone he'd rather spend it on than Grace.

Guess that wasn't happening. A grown-up field trip didn't sound too much like Grace's definition of *slow* anyway, so it hardly mattered that his half-formed plan wasn't going to work out.

No matter. He'd spend the weekend with his daughters and it would be great. They'd bond and his love for them would grow. Maybe this was actually a good step toward relieving Hadley permanently of her baby duties. He could keep telling himself that she loved them and didn't mind taking care of his daughters all he wanted, but at the end of the day, it was just an excuse.

He'd decided to stay in Royal, taking a job managing the cattle side of Wade Ranch, and it was time for him to man up and start building the family life his daughters needed.

Liam and Hadley left in a flurry of instructions and worried backward glances until finally Kyle was alone with Maddie and Maggie. That little pang in his stomach was back and he pushed on it with his thumb. The feeling didn't go away and started resembling panic more than anything else.

God Almighty. Maddie and Maggie were babies, for crying out loud. Kyle had faced down a high-ranking, card-carrying member of the Taliban with less sweat.

He wandered into the nursery and thought about covering his eyes to shield them from all the pink. But there his girls were. Two of 'em. Staring up at him with the slightly unfocused, slightly bemused expression his daughters seemed to favor. The babies were kind of sweet when they weren't crying.

They couldn't lie around in their room all night.

"Let's hang out," he announced to his kids. It had a nice ring.

He gathered up Maggie from her crib and carried her downstairs to the family room, where a conglomeration of baby paraphernalia sat in the corner. He dragged one of the baby seats away from the wall with one bare foot and placed Maggie in it the way Hadley always did. There were some straps, similar to a parachute harness, and he grabbed one of Maggie's waving fists to thread it through the arm hole.

She promptly clocked him with the other one, which earned a laugh even as his cheek started smarting. "That's what I get for taking my eye off the ball, right?"

The noise she made didn't sound too much like agreement, but he nodded anyway, as if they were having a conversation. That was one of the things Hadley said all the time. The babies were people, not aliens. He could talk to them normally and it helped increase their vocabulary later on if everyone got out of the habit of using baby talk around them.

Which was fine by Kyle. Baby talk was dumb anyway.

Once Maggie was secured, he fetched Maddie and repeated the process. That was the thing about twins. You were never done. One of them always needed something, and then the other one needed the same thing or something different or both.

But here they were, having family time. In the family room. Couldn't get more domestic than that. He sat on the couch and looked at his daughters squirming in their bouncy seats. Now what?

"You ladies want to watch some TV?"

Since neither one of them started wailing at the suggestion, he took it as a yes.

The flat-screen television mounted to the wall blinked on with a flick of the remote. Kyle tuned to one of the kids' channels, where a group of grown men in bright colors were singing a song about a dog named Wags. The song was almost horrifying in its simplicity and in the dancing that would probably lace his nightmares later that night, assuming he actually slept while continually reliving that aborted kiss with Grace from earlier.

The babies both turned their little faces to the TV and for all intents and purposes looked as though they were watching it. Hadley had said they couldn't really make out stuff really well yet, because their eyes weren't developed enough to know what they were looking at, but they could still enjoy the colors and lights.

And that's when Maddie started fussing. Loudly.

Kyle pulled her out of her baby seat, cursing his burning hands, which were still raw from his climb out of the ravine. Liam's timing sucked. "Shh, little one. That's no way to talk to your daddy."

She cried harder. It was only a matter of time before Maggie got jealous of the attention and set about getting some of her own with a few well-placed sobs. Hadley could usually ignore it but Kyle didn't have her stamina.

Plan A wasn't working. Kyle rocked his daughter faster but she only cried harder. And there was no one to help analyze the symptoms in order to arrive at a potential solution. This was a solo operation. So he'd run it to completion.

Bottle. That was always Plan B, after rocking. It was close to dinnertime. Kyle secured Maddie in the chair again, forced to let her wail while he fixed her bottle. It seemed cruel, but he needed both hands.

He'd seen some guys wear a baby sling. But he couldn't quite bring himself to go that far, and he'd never seen Liam do it, either, so there was justification for holding on to his dude card, albeit slight.

Maddie sucked the bottle dry quicker than a baby calf who'd lost its mama. Kyle burped her and resettled her in her bouncy seat, intending to move on to Maggie, who was likely wondering where her bottle was.

Maddie was having none of that and let loose with another round of wails.

In desperation, he sang his go-to Taylor Swift song, which surprisingly worked well enough to ease his pounding headache. He sang the verse over again and slid into the chorus with gusto. The moment he stopped, she set off again, louder. He sang. She quieted. He stopped. She cried.

"Maddie," he groaned. "Tim McGraw should have been your daddy if this is how you're going to be. I can't sing 24-7."

More crying. With more mercy than he probably deserved, Maggie had been sitting quietly in her seat the whole time, but things surely wouldn't stay so peaceful on her end.

Feeling like the world's biggest idiot, he sneaked off to the kitchen to call Hadley. There was no way on God's green earth he'd call Liam, but Hadley was another story.

She answered on the first ring. "Is everything okay?"

"Fine, fine," he assured her, visualizing Liam throwing their overnight bags into the cockpit of the Cessna and flying off toward home without even pausing to shut the door. "Well, except Maddie won't stop crying. I've tried everything, bottle, rocking, and it's a bust. Any ideas?"

"Did you burp her?"

"Of course." He hadn't changed her diaper, but his sense of smell was pretty good and he didn't think that was the problem.

"Temperature?"

He dashed back into the family room, cringing at the decibel level of Maddie's cries, and put a hand on her forehead. Which was moronic when he'd been holding her for thirty minutes. "She doesn't feel hot."

"Is that Maddie crying like that?" Now Hadley sounded worried, which was not what Kyle had intended. "Take her temperature anyway, just to be sure. Then try the gas drops. Call me back in an hour and let me know how it's going."

"Won't I be interrupting?" He so did not want to know the answer to that, but it was pretty crappy of him to call once, let alone twice.

"Yes," Liam growled in the background. "Stop coddling him, Hadley."

Kyle muttered an expletive aimed at Liam, but his wife was the one who heard it. "Excuse my French, Hadley.

Never mind. I got this. You and Liam go back to whatever you were doing, which I do *not* need details about."

"We should come home," Hadley interjected. This was accompanied by a very vehement "No!" from Liam, and some muffled conversation. "Okay, we're not coming home. You'll be fine," Hadley said into the phone in her soothing voice that she normally reserved for the girls, but whether it was directed at Liam or Kyle, he couldn't say. "Call Clare if you need to. She won't mind."

"Clare?" Liam's incredulity came through loud and clear despite his mouth being nowhere near the phone. "She's already got plenty of babies that Royal Memorial pays her to take care of. Call Grace if you're going to call anyone."

Grace. He could get Grace over here under the guise of helping with the twins and get to see her tonight after all. Now that was a stellar idea if Kyle had ever heard one. Not that he was about to let Liam get all cocky about it. "Sorry I bothered you. Good night."

Kyle eyed the still-screaming baby. Fatherhood wasn't a job for the fainthearted, that was for sure. Nor was it a job for the clueless, and thankfully, Ms. Haines already had him cast in her head as such. She thought he was clueless? Great.

Time to use that to his advantage.

Eight

When the phone rang, Grace almost didn't answer it.

The oven had freaked out. Worse than last time. It turned on and heated up fine, but halfway through the cooking cycle, the element shut off. Cold. Which described the state of her dinner, too. The roast was still raw inside and she could have used the potatoes to pound nails.

But there was no saving it now. The oven wouldn't start again no matter how much she cursed at it. She'd checked the power cord but it was plugged in with no visible frays or anything. Last time, she'd been able to turn it off and turn it back on, but that didn't work this time.

So why not answer the phone?

Except it was Kyle. His name flashed at her from the screen and she stared at it for a moment as the *wow* from earlier flooded all her full-grown woman parts. So this was taking it slow? Calling her mere hours after she'd broken off a kiss with more willpower than it should have taken—for the second time?

"This better be important," she said instead of hello, and then winced. Her mama had raised her better than that.

"It is." Something that sounded like a tornado siren wailed in the distance. "Something's wrong with Maddie."

That was *Maddie* doing the siren impression? *Relapse.* Her heart rate sped up. Those harrowing hours when they didn't know what was wrong with Maddie came back in a rush. Heart problems were no joke, and Maddie'd had several surgeries to correct the abnormalities.

"What's wrong? Where's Hadley?" She might be hyperventilating. Was that what it was called when you couldn't breathe?

"She and Liam went to Vail. I didn't want to bother them."

Vail? Suspicion ruffled the edges of Grace's consciousness. The couple had just gone to Vail a couple of months ago. Was this some kind of covert attempt to get Kyle to take his fatherhood responsibilities more seriously? Or an elaborate setup from the mind of Kyle Wade to get his way with Grace?

"Okay," she said slowly, feeling her way through the land mines. "Did you try—"

"Yep. I tried everything. She's been crying like this for an hour and it's upsetting Maggie. I wouldn't have called you otherwise." He was trying hard to keep the panic from his voice, but she could tell he was at the end of his rope. Her heart melted a little, sweeping aside all her suspicion.

It didn't matter why Liam and Hadley had gone to Vail. Maddie—and Kyle—needed help, and she couldn't ignore that for anything.

"Do you need me to come by?" She shouldn't, for all the reasons she hadn't stayed with him in the barn earlier that day.

Plus, and this was the kicker, he hadn't asked her to come over. Maybe it was supposed to be implied, but this was typical with Kyle. He had a huge problem just coming out and saying what he thought. That might be the number one reason she hadn't stayed in his arms, both back in high school and today.

Nothing had changed.

"That's a great idea," he said enthusiastically, and she didn't miss that he was acting as though it was all hers, and not what he'd been after the whole time. "I'll cook you dinner as a thank-you. Unless you've got other plans?"

Ha. If she couldn't hear Maddie's cries for herself, she'd think he'd set all this up. Grace glanced at her oven and half-cooked dinner, then at the lonely dining room table where she'd eaten a lot of meals by herself, especially in the past three years upon becoming a Professional Single Girl.

The timing was oh, so convenient. But even Kyle couldn't magically make her oven stop working at precisely the moment he'd asked her to come over for dinner. Thus far she'd avoided having any meals with him and his family because that would be too hard. Too much of a reminder that a husband and children was what she wanted more than anything—and that there was nothing on the horizon to indicate she'd ever get either one.

But this was an emergency. Or at least that was what she was going to keep telling herself.

"I'll be right there," she promised, and dumped the roast in the trash. If she freshened up her makeup and put on a different dress, no one had to know.

She drove to Wade Ranch at four miles per hour over the speed limit.

Kyle opened the door before she knocked. "Hey, Grace. Thanks."

His pure physical beauty swept out and slapped her. Mute, she stared at his face, memorizing it, which was silly when she already had a handy image of him, shirtless, emblazoned across her brain. She'd just seen him a few hours ago. Why did she have to have a reaction by simply standing near him?

"Where's Maddie?" she asked brusquely to cover the catch in her throat.

"Right this way, Ms. Haines."

Grace followed Kyle through the formal parlor and across the hardwood floor into the hall connecting to the back of the house. Why did it feel like the blind leading the blind? She didn't have any special baby knowledge. Most kids in the system were older by the time their cases landed on her desk, which brought back her earlier reservations about the real reason he'd called her. It wouldn't be the first time today that he'd manufactured a scenario to get a reaction from her.

In the family room, two babies sat in low seats, wide-eyed as they stared at the TV, both silent as the grave.

Grace pointed out the obvious. "Um. Maddie's not crying."

"I gave her Tylenol while you were on your way over here." He shrugged. "Must have worked."

"Why didn't you call me?"

"She didn't stop crying until a few minutes before you got here," he replied defensively, which was only fair. She'd heard Maddie crying over the phone. It wasn't as if he'd shoved Liam and Hadley out the door, and then faked an emergency to get her into his clutches.

She sighed. "I'm sorry. I'm being rude. It's just… I was convinced this was all just an elaborate plot to get me to have dinner with you."

Kyle blinked. "Why on earth would I do that?"

"Well, you know." Discomfort prickled the back of her neck as he stared at her in pure confusion. "Because you faked all that stuff with Emma Jane earlier today. Seemed like it might be a trend."

He cocked his head and gave her a small smile. "I called

you because it was the best of both worlds. I needed help with Maddie and I wanted to see you, too. Is that so terrible?"

Not when he put it that way. Chagrined, she shook her head. "No. But it just seems like I'm a little extraneous at this point. I should probably go. Maddie's fine."

"Don't be silly." His smile faltered just a touch. "She might go off again at any moment and Maggie could decide to join in. What will I do then? Please stay. Besides, I promised you dinner. Let me do something nice for you for coming all this way."

The panicky undercurrent had climbed back into his voice, bless his heart. She couldn't help but smile in hopes of bolstering his confidence. "It wasn't that far. But okay. I'll stay."

"Great. It's settled then." He held out his hand as if he wanted to shake on it but when she placed her hand in his, he yanked on it, pulling her toward the bouncy seats. "Come on, grab a baby and you can watch me cook."

Laughing, she did as commanded, though he insisted on taking Maddie himself. She gathered up Maggie, bouncy seat and all, and followed him to the kitchen, mirroring his moves as he situated the seat near one of the two islands in the center of the room, presumably so the girls didn't feel left out.

She kissed Maggie on the head, unable to resist her sweet face. This baby was special for lots of reasons, but mostly because of who her daddy was.

Wow. Where had that come from? She needed to reel it back, pronto.

"We'll let them hang out for a little while," Kyle said conversationally. "And then we'll put them to bed. Hadley has them on a strict schedule."

"Sure. I'd be glad to help."

It sounded great, actually. The children she helped always either had families already, or were waiting on her to find them the best one. Grace never got to keep any of the children on whose behalf she worked, which was a little heartbreaking in a way.

But here she was, right in the middle of Maddie and Maggie's permanent home, spending time with them and their father outside of work. The smell of baby powder clung to her hands where she'd picked up Maggie, and all at once, soft jazz music floated through the kitchen as Kyle clicked up an internet radio station at the kitchen's entertainment center. It was a bit magical and her throat tightened.

This was not her life. She didn't trust Kyle enough to consider where this could lead. But all at once, she couldn't remember why that was so important. All she had to do right this minute was enjoy this.

"Can I do something to help with dinner?" she asked, since the babies were occupied with staring at their fists.

Kyle grinned and pulled a stool from behind the island, pointing to it. "Sit. Your job is to keep me company."

Charmed, she watched as instructed. It wasn't a hardship. He moved fluidly, as comfortable sliding a bottle from the built-in wine refrigerator as he was handling the reins of his mount earlier that day.

The cork gave way with a *pop* and he poured her a glass of pale yellow wine, handing it to her with one finger in the universal "one minute" gesture. He grabbed his own glass and clinked it against hers. "To bygones."

She raised a brow. That was an interesting thing to toast to. But appropriate. She was determined not to let the past interfere with her family moment, and the future was too murky. "To bygones."

They both drank from their glasses, staring at each other over the rims, and she had the distinct impression he was evaluating her just as much as she was him.

The fruity tang of the wine raced across her tongue, cool and delicious. And unexpected. "I wouldn't have pegged you as a Chardonnay kind of guy," she commented.

"I'm full of surprises." With that cryptic comment, he set his wineglass on the counter and began pulling items from the double-doored stainless steel refrigerator. "I'm making something simple. Chicken salad. I hope that's okay. The ladies didn't give me a lot of time to prep."

She hid a smile at his description of the babies. "Sounds great."

Kyle bustled around the kitchen chopping lettuce and a cooked chicken breast, leaving her to alternate watching him and the twins. Though he drew her eye far more than she would have expected, given that she was here to help with the babies.

"I don't remember you being much of a connoisseur in the kitchen," she said as he began mixing the ingredients for homemade dressing.

They'd been so young the first time, though. Not even out of their teens, yet their twenties were practically in the rearview mirror now. Of course they'd grown and changed. It would be more shocking if they hadn't.

"In a place like Afghanistan, if you don't learn to cook, you starve," he returned.

It was rare for him to mention his military stint, and it occurred to her that she typically shied away from the subject because it held so many negative associations. For her, at least. He might feel differently about the thing that had taken him away from her, and she was suddenly curious about it.

"Did you enjoy being in the military?"

He glanced up, his expression shuttered all at once. "It was a part of me. And now it's not."

Okay, message received. He didn't want to talk about that. Which was fine. Neither did she.

"I'm at a stopping point," he said, his tone a little lighter. "Let's put the girls to bed."

Though she suspected it was merely a diversion, she nodded and followed him through the mysterious ritual of bedtime. It was over before she'd fully immersed herself in the moment. They changed the girls' diapers, changed their outfits, put them down on their backs and left the room.

"That was it?" she whispered as she and Kyle took the back stairs to the kitchen.

"Yep. Sometimes Hadley rocks them if they don't go to sleep right away, but she says not to do that too much, or they'll get used to it, and we'll be doing it until they go to college." He waved the mobile video monitor in his hand. "I watch and listen using this and if they fuss, I come running. Not much more to it."

They emerged into the kitchen, where the tangy scent of the salad dressing greeted them. Kyle set the monitor on the counter on his way to the area where he'd been preparing dinner.

He'd clearly been asking Hadley questions and soaking up her baby knowledge. Much more so than Grace would have given him credit for. "You're taking fatherhood very seriously."

He halted and whirled so fast that she smacked into his chest. But he didn't step back. "What's it going to take to convince you that I'm in this for the long haul?"

Blinking, she stared up into his green eyes as they cut through her. Condemning her. Uncertain all of a sudden, she tried to take a step back, but he didn't let her. His hands shot out to grip her elbows, hauling her back into place. Into his space. A hairbreadth from the cut torso she'd felt under her fingers earlier today.

"What will it take, Grace?" he murmured. "You say something like that and it makes me think you're surprised that I'm ready, willing and able to take care of my daughters. *Still* surprised, after all I've done and learned. After I've become gainfully employed. After I've shown you my commitment in site visits like you asked. This isn't about me anymore. It's about you. Why is this all so hard for you to believe?"

"Because, Kyle!" she burst out. "You've been gone. You didn't come home when Liam called you about the babies. Is it so difficult to fathom that I might have questions about your intentions? You just said the military was a part of you. What if you wake up one day and want to join up again? Those girls will suffer."

I'd suffer.

Where had that come from? She tried to shake it off, but as they stood there in the kitchen of Wade House with his masculinity pouring over her like a hot wind from the south, the emotions welled up again and she cursed herself. Cursed the truth.

Sometime between his coming home and now, she'd opened her heart again. Just a little. She'd tried to stop, tried asking for space, but the honest truth was that she'd never gotten over him because she still had feelings for him. And it had only taken one kiss to awaken them again, no matter how much she'd tried to lie to herself about it. Otherwise, that scene with Emma Jane would have rolled right off like water from a duck's back.

And she didn't trust him not to hurt her again. It was a terrible place to be stuck.

"Grace," he murmured. "I'm here. For good. I didn't get Liam's messages, or I would have been back earlier. You've got me cast in your head as someone with my sights set on the horizon, but that's not true. I want to live my life in Royal, at least until my daughters are grown."

He wasn't aiming to leave the moment he changed his mind. He was telling the truth; she could see it in his eyes.

Maybe she wasn't such a bad judge of character after all. Maybe she could let her guard down. Just a little.

The tightness in her throat relaxed and she took the first easy breath since smacking into him. "Okay. I'll shut up about it."

"Just to make sure, let me help you shut up."

He hauled her up and kissed her. His mouth took hers at a hard, desperate angle that she instantly responded to. Maybe she didn't have to resist if he wasn't going to leave again. Maybe she didn't have to pretend she didn't want more. Because he was right here, giving it to her. All she had to do was take it.

His hands were still on her elbows, raising her up on her tiptoes as he devoured her with his unique whole-body kiss. Need unfolded inside, seeking relief, seeking Kyle.

Yes. The darkness she sometimes sensed in him lifted as he dropped her elbows to encompass her in his arms, holding her tight. He backed her up against the counter to press his hard body to hers, thrusting his hips to increase the contact.

A moan bloomed in her chest, and her tongue vibrated against his as he took the kiss deeper, sliding a hand down her back, to her waist, to her bottom, molding it to fit in his palm. His touch thrilled her even as she pressed into it, willing him to spread the wealth. And then he did.

His hand went lower, gripping the back of her thigh, lifting it so that her knee came up flush with his thigh, which hiked her dress up, and *oh, my.* She was open to him under her skirt, flimsy panties the only barrier between her damp center and his very hard body.

He thrust his hips again, igniting her instantly as the rough fabric of his jeans pleasured her through the scrap of fabric at her core. Strung tight, she let the dense heat wash through her, mindless with it as she sought more. His mouth lifted from hers for a moment and she nearly wept, following him involuntarily with her lips in hopes of reclaiming the drugging kiss.

"Grace," he murmured, and dragged his lips across her throat to the hollow near her ear, which was so nice, she forgot about kissing and let her head tip back to give him better access.

He spent a long moment exploring the area, and finally nipped her ear lightly, whispering, "You know, when I said I wanted to live my life in Royal, I didn't picture myself alone."

"I hope not," she murmured. "You have two daughters."

He laughed softly, as she'd intended, and hefted her a little deeper into his arms as he lifted his head to meet her gaze. "You know that's not what I meant."

Of course she did. But was it so difficult to spell out what was going on his head? So difficult to say how he felt about her? She wanted to hear the words. This time, she wasn't settling for less than everything. "Tell me what you're picturing, Kyle."

"Me. You." He slid light fingertips down the sweetheart neckline of her dress until he reached the spot right between her breasts and hooked the fabric. "This dress on the floor."

Shuddering in spite of herself at the heated desire in his expression, she smiled. "Let's pretend for argument's sake I'm in favor of this dress on the floor. What would you say to me while you're peeling it off?"

The glint in his eye set off another shower of sparks in her midsection. "Well, my darling. Why don't we just find out?"

Slowly, he pulled down the shoulders of the dress, baring her bra straps, which he promptly gathered up, as well. She heartily blessed the impulse that had caused her to pick this semibackless dress that didn't require unzipping to get out of. Which might not have been an accident.

"Beautiful." He kissed a shoulder, suckling on it lightly, then following her neckline with the little nibbling kisses until she thought she'd come apart from the torture.

When she'd asked him to talk about what was on his mind, she'd been expecting a declaration of his feelings. This was so much better. For now.

All at once, the dress and bra popped down to her waist in a big bunch of fabric, baring her breasts to his hot-eyed viewing pleasure. And look he did, shamelessly, as if he'd uncovered a diamond he couldn't quite believe was real.

"Grace," he rasped. "Exactly like I remembered in my dreams. But so much more."

That pleased her enormously for some reason. It was much more romantic than what she recalled him saying when they were together ten years ago. He'd seen her naked before, but always in semidarkness, and usually in his truck. Bench seats were not the height of romance.

With a reverent curse, he brushed one nipple with his thumb, and her breath whooshed from her lungs as everything went tight inside. And outside.

"Kyle," she said, and nearly strangled on the word as he lifted her up onto the counter, spreading her legs and stepping between them. Then his mouth closed over a breast and she forgot how to speak as he sucked, flicking her nipple with his tongue simultaneously.

She forgot everything except the exquisite feel of this man's mouth on her body.

Her head fell back as he pushed a hand against the small of her back to arch her toward his mouth, drawing her breast deeper into it. She moaned, writhing with pleasure as the heat swept over her entire body, swirling at her core. Where she needed him most.

As if he'd read her mind, his other hand toyed with her panties until she felt his fingers touching her intimately. It was cataclysmic, perfect. Until he placed his thumb on her nub, expertly rubbing as he pleasured her, and that was even more perfect. Heat at her core, suction at her breast, and it all coalesced in one bright, hot pinnacle. With a cry, she crested in a long orgasm of epic proportions.

She'd just had an *orgasm* on the *kitchen counter*. She should probably be more embarrassed about that...

Before she'd fully recovered, Kyle picked her up from the counter and let her slide to the floor, then hustled her up the stairs to a bedroom. Heavy, masculine furnishings dominated the room, marking it as his, but a few leftover items from his youth still decorated the walls. He dimmed the light and advanced on her with his slow, lazy walk.

"Oh, there's more?" she teased.

"So much more," he growled. "It's been far too long since I've felt you under me. I want you naked. Now."

That sounded like a plan. The warm-up in the kitchen had only gotten her good and primed for what came next.

Breathless, she stood still as he peeled her dress the rest of the way from her body and let it fall to the carpet. She promptly forgot to worry about the extra pounds she'd gained in her hips and thighs since the last time he'd seen her.

He stripped off his shirt, exposing that beautiful torso she'd barely had time to explore earlier.

When his jeans hit the floor, she realized his chest was only part of the package, and the rest—*oh, my*. He turned slightly, holding one leg behind him at an odd angle, almost as if he was posing for her. Well, okay then. Greedily, she looked her fill, returning the favor from earlier when he'd gorged on the sight of her bare breasts.

In the low light, he was quite simply gorgeous, with muscles bulging in his thighs and a jutting erection that spoke of his passion more effectively than anything he could have said. The power of it coursed through her. She was a woman in the company of a finely built man who was here with the sole intent of pleasuring her with that cut, solid body. And she got to do the same to him.

Why had she waited so long for this?

"Grace."

She glanced up into his eyes, which were so hot, she felt the burn across her uncovered skin, heightening her desire to *get started* already. He was going to feel amazing.

"You have to stop looking at me like that," he rasped.

"Because why?"

He chuckled weakly. "Because this is going to be all over in about two seconds if you don't. I want to take my time with you. Savor you."

"Maybe you can do that the second time," she suggested, a little shocked at her boldness, but not sorry. "I'm okay with you going fast the first time if I get to look at you however much I want. Oh, and there's going to be touching, too."

To prove the point, she reached out to trace the line of his pectoral muscles, because how could she not? He groaned under her fingertips and that was so nice, she flattened her palms against his chest. "More," she commanded.

He raised his eyebrows. "When did you get so bossy?"

"Five minutes ago." When she'd realized she was a woman with desires. And she wanted this man. Why shouldn't she get to call a few shots?

With a small push at his torso, she shoved him toward the bed. And to his credit, he let her, because there was no way she'd have moved him otherwise. He fell backward onto the bed and she climbed on to kneel next to him, a little uncertain where to start. But determined to figure it out.

"Just be still," she told him as he stared up at her with question marks in his gaze. Then she got busy exploring.

What would he taste like? There was only one way to find out. She leaned down and ran her tongue across his nipple, and it was as delicious as she'd expected. He hissed as the underlying muscle jerked.

"Staying still is easier said than done when you're doing that," he muttered, his voice cracking as she ran her tongue lower, down his abs and to his thigh.

She eyed his erection and, curious, reached out to touch it. Hard and soft at the same time, it pulsed against her palm.

He cursed. "Playtime's over."

Instantly, he rolled her under him in one fierce move, taking her mouth in a searing kiss that rendered her boneless. She melted into the comforter as he shoved a leg between hers, rubbing at her core until she was in flames.

He paused only for a moment to sheathe himself with a condom, and then nudged her legs open to ease into her slowly.

Gasping as he filled her, she clung to his shoulders, reveling in the feel of him. This was so different than she remembered. The experience was so much stronger and bigger. The leftover emotion that she'd carried with her for the past ten years exploded into something she barely recognized. Before, Kyle had been in a compartment in her mind, in her heart. Something she could take out and remember, then put back when she got sad.

There was no putting this back in a box.

The essence of Kyle swept through her, filling every nook and cranny of her body and soul. No, he hadn't bubbled over with lots of pretty words about being in love with her. But that would come, in time. She had to believe that.

And then he buried himself completely with a groan. They were so intimately joined, Grace could feel his heartbeat throughout her whole body. They moved in tandem, mutually seeking to increase the pleasure, spiraling higher toward the heavens, and she lost all track of time and place as they lost themselves in each other.

The rhythms were familiar, like dancing to the same song so often you memorized the moves. But the familiarity only heightened the experience because she didn't have to wonder what would happen next.

Just as he'd done when they'd been together before, he stared into her eyes as he loved her, refusing to let her look away. Opening his soul to her as they joined again and again. The romance of it swept through her and she held him close.

This was why she'd fallen in love with him. Why she'd never had even the slightest desire to do this with any other man. He made her feel that she completed him without saying a word. Sure, she wanted the words. But times like this made them unnecessary.

Before she was fully ready for it to end, his urgency increased, sending her into an oblivion of sensation until she climaxed, and then he followed her into the light, holding her tight against him as they soared.

She lay there engulfed in his arms, wishing she never had to move from this spot.

Kyle must have been reading her mind, because he murmured in her ear, "Stay. All weekend."

"I don't have any of my stuff," she said lamely as reality nosed its way into the perfect moment.

"Go get a bag and come back."

It was a reasonable suggestion. But then what? Were they jumping back into their relationship as if nothing had happened and ten years hadn't passed? As if they'd dealt with the hurt and separation?

That was too much reality. She sat up and his arms fell away to rest on the comforter.

"I see the wheels turning," he commented mildly as he pulled a sheet over his lower half in a strange bout of modesty. "This is a beginning, Grace. Let's see where it takes us. Don't throw up any more walls."

She shut her eyes. Romance was great, but there was so much more that she wanted in a relationship. There'd been no declarations of undying love. No marriage proposal. Why did he get a pass that no other man got? She was caught between her inescapable feelings for Kyle and her standards.

And the intense hope that things might be different this time.

How would she ever find out if she left?

"Okay." She nodded and ignored the hammering of her pulse. "Let's see where it goes."

Nine

Kyle waited on Grace to come back by pretending to watch TV.

His body had cooled—on the outside—but the inside was still pretty keyed up. He wasn't really interested in much of anything other than getting Grace back in his bed, but this time for the whole night.

When the crunch of gravel sounded outside, breath he hadn't realized he'd been holding whooshed out. She'd come back.

He met Grace at the door, opening it wide as she climbed the front porch steps, her hair still mussed from their thorough lovemaking of less than an hour ago. Her face shone in the porch light, so beautiful and fresh, and his chest hitched as he soaked in the sight of her.

"Hey, Grace," he said, pretty dang happy his voice still worked.

He'd wondered if she might back out, call and say she'd changed her mind. She was still so skittish. She might have let him into her body but he didn't fool himself for a second that she'd let him into her head, or her heart. It wasn't the way it had been, when he'd been her hero, her everything. There was distance now that hadn't been there before and he didn't like it.

Of course, some of that was his fault. Not much. But a little. He didn't fully trust her, and while he'd sworn in theory to forget about the past, it was proving more difficult to do in practice than he'd thought it would be, so he didn't press the issue of the yawning chasm between them.

"Hey." She had a bag slung over her shoulder and a shy smile on her face.

Shy? After the temptress she'd been? It caught him up short. Maybe some of the distance was due to sheer unfamiliarity between them. As comfortable as *he* felt around Grace, that didn't mean she was totally in the groove yet. Plus, they didn't know each other as well as they used to. Ten years didn't vanish just because two people slept together.

"We never had dinner," he commented. "Come sit with me and we'll eat. For real this time."

She nodded and let him take her bag, following him to the table where he laid out silverware and refilled their wineglasses. They ate the chicken salad and polished off the bottle of wine, chatting long after clearing their plates. Grace told cute stories about the children on her case docket, and Kyle reciprocated with some carefully selected anecdotes about the guys he'd trained with in Coronado during BUD/S. Carefully selected because that period had been among the toughest of his life as his training honed him into an elite warrior—*while* he was fighting his own internal battle against the hurt this woman had caused. But he'd survived and wasn't dwelling on that.

Couldn't dwell on it. Liam wasn't a factor and he wanted

to do things with Grace differently this time. And by the time Kyle was done with her, she'd be asking, "Liam who?"

A wail over the monitor drew their attention away from their conversation and Grace gladly helped him get the girls settled again. It was nearing midnight; hopefully it would be the only time the babies woke up for the night.

Kyle didn't mind rolling out of bed at any hour to take care of his daughters, but he selfishly wanted to spend the rest of the night with Grace, and Grace alone. He got his wish. They fell asleep wrapped in each other's arms, and Kyle slept like the dead until dawn.

His eyes snapped open and he took a half second to orient. Not a SEAL. Not in Afghanistan. But with *Grace*. A blessing to count, among many.

Until he tried to snuggle her closer. White-hot pokers of pain shot through his busted leg as he rolled. He bit back the curse and breathed through it.

The pain hadn't been so bad last night, but of course, he'd been pretty distracted. Plus, he normally soaked his leg before going to bed but hadn't had a chance last night. Apparently, he was going to pay for it today.

All the commotion woke Grace.

"Good morning," she murmured sleepily, and slid a leg along his, which was simultaneously arousing and excruciating.

"Wait," he said hoarsely.

"Don't wanna." She stretched provocatively, rubbing her bare breasts against his chest, which distracted him enough that he didn't realize she'd hooked her knee around his leg. She fairly purred with sexy little sounds that meant she was turned on. And probably about to do something about it.

"Grace." He grabbed her shoulders and squared them so he could be sure he had her attention. "Stop."

Her expression went from hot and sleepy to confused

and guarded. Her whole body stiffened, pulling away from his. "Okay. Sorry."

"No, don't be sorry." Kyle swore. *Moron*. He was mucking this up and all he wanted to do was pull her back against him. Dive in, distract himself. But he couldn't. "Listen."

He took a deep breath, fighting the pain, fighting his instinct to clam up again.

He hadn't told anyone about what had happened to him in Afghanistan and didn't want to start with the woman who still had the power to declare him an unfit parent if he admitted to having a busted leg. But as he stared into her troubled brown eyes, his heart lurched and he had to come clean. This was part of closing that distance between them. Part of learning to trust her again.

She'd said she was going to let him keep his girls. He had to believe her. Believe *in* her, or this was never going to work, not now, not in a hundred years.

"I didn't tell you to stop because I wanted you to."

Her gaze softened along with her body. "Then what's going on, Kyle?"

"I got wounded," he muttered. Which made him sound as much like a wuss as he felt. "Overseas."

"Oh, I didn't know!" She gasped and drew back to glance down the length of his body, her expression darkening gorgeously as she took in his semiaroused state. "You don't *look* wounded. Everything I see is quite nice."

And now it was a fully aroused state. Fantastic. This was so not a conversation he wanted to have in the first place, let alone with a hard-on. "My leg. The bone was shattered. I had a lot of surgeries and they put most of it back together. But it still hurts, especially in the morning when I haven't stretched it."

Sympathy poured from her gaze as she sat up and pulled the sheet back, gathering it up in her hand as she sought the scar. When she found it along the far side of his calf, she touched the skin just above it lightly with her fingers. "You hid this last night. With the low light and striking that weird pose. Why didn't you tell me?"

"It's…"

How to explain the horror of being wounded in the line of duty? It wasn't just the pain and the fact that he wasn't ever going to be the same again, but he'd been unable to protect the rest of his team. He'd been unable to *do his job* because his leg didn't work all at once. A SEAL got back up when he was knocked down. *Every time.* Only Kyle hadn't.

Maybe he'd fail at being a parent, too, because of it. That was his worst fear.

"I don't like being weak," he finally said, which was true, if not the whole truth. "I don't like giving you ammunition to take away Maddie and Maggie. Like I might not be a good daddy because my leg doesn't work right."

"Oh, Kyle." She laid her lips on the scar for a moment, and the light touch seared his heart. "I would never take away your daughters because of an injury. That's ridiculous."

He shrugged, unable to meet her gaze. "You were going to take them away because I didn't come home for two months. But I was in the hospital."

"Well, you could have said that!" Exasperation spurted out with the phrase and she shook her head. "For crying out loud. Am I supposed to be a mind reader?"

Yes. Then he wouldn't have to figure out how to say things that were too hard.

"Now you know," he mumbled instead. "That's why I had to stop earlier. Not because I wasn't on board. I just needed a minute."

"Okay." But then she smiled and ran a hand up his thigh,

dangerously close to his erection. "It's been a minute. How about we try this instead, now that I know?"

The protest got caught in his throat as she rolled him onto his back and crawled over him, careful not to touch his leg, but deliberately letting her breasts and long curls brush his skin from thigh to chest. She captured his wrists and encircled them with her fingers, drawing his arms above his head, holding them in place as her hips undulated.

"What are you doing?" His voice scraped the lower register as she ignited his flesh with her sexy movements.

She arched a brow. "Really? I should hope it would be fairly obvious. Since it's not, shut up and I'll make it clearer for you."

He did as advised because his tongue was stuck to the roof of his mouth anyway. And then she leaned forward, still holding his wrists hostage, and kissed him. Hot. Open-mouthed. The kind of kiss laden with dark promise and he eagerly lapped it up. He could break free of her finger shackles easily, but why the hell would he do that?

She had him right where she wanted him, apparently, and since he could find no complaint with it, he let her have the floor. She experimented with different angles of her head as she kissed him, looking for something unknown and he went along for the ride, groaning with the effort it took to hold back.

Then she trailed her mouth down his throat, nipped at his earlobe and writhed against his erection all at once, slicing a long, hot knife of need through his groin. His hips strained toward hers, rocking involuntarily as he sought relief, and he started to pull his arms loose so he could roll her under him to get this show on the road. But she shook her head and tightened her grip on his wrists.

"No, sir," she admonished with a wicked smile. "You're not permitted to do anything but lie there."

This was going to kill him. Flat out stop his heart.

He got what she was doing. She wanted him to keep his leg still, while she did all the dirty work. Something tender hooked his heart as he stared up at her, poised over him with an all-business look on her face that was somehow endearing.

But he wasn't an invalid.

"I hate to break it to you, darling, but that's not happening." He flexed his hips again, sliding his erection against her bare, damp sex, watching as her eyes unfocused with pleasure. "I suggest you think about how you're going to get a condom on me with your hands occupied because I'm going to be inside you in about point two seconds."

"Don't ruin this for me." She mock-pouted and promptly crossed his wrists, one over the other, and held on with one hand as she wiggled the fingers of her free hand in a cheery wave. "I always dreamed of being a rodeo star. This is my chance."

He had to laugh, which downright ached. All over. "That's what's on your mind right now? Rodeo?"

"Oh, yeah." She leaned against his abs, holding on with her thighs as she fished around in the nightstand drawer and pulled out a condom, which she held up triumphantly. "I'm going for a ten in the bucking bronco event."

"I'll be the judge of that," he quipped, and then raised a brow at the condom. "Go ahead. I'm waiting."

In the end, she had to let go of his arms to rip open the foil package. But he obediently held his wrists above his head as she had so sweetly asked. Then there was no more talking as she eased over him, taking him gently in her hands to pleasure him as she rolled on the condom.

He groaned as need broke over him in a wave, and then she slowly guided him into her damp heat. He slid all the way in as she pushed downward and it was unbelievable. They joined and it was better than it had been last night.

Deeper. More amazing, because there were no more secrets between them.

She knew about his injury and hadn't run screaming
for her report to revise it. She hadn't been repulsed by his
weaknesses. Instead, she'd somehow twisted it around so
they could make love without hurting his leg. It was sweet
and wonderful.

And then she got busy on her promise to turn him into a
bucking bronco, sliding up and down, rolling her hips and
generally driving him mad with want. He obliged her by
letting his body go with the sensation, meeting her thrusts
and driving them both higher until she came with a little
cry and he followed her.

Clutching her to his chest, he breathed in tandem with
her, still joined and not anxious to change that. He held
her hot body to his because he didn't think he could let go.

"You're amazing," he murmured into her hair, and she
turned her head to lay her cheek on his shoulder, a pleased
smile on her face.

"I wouldn't say no to thank-you flowers."

He made a mental note to send her a hundred roses the
moment his bones returned and he could actually move.
"Where'd you get that sexy little hip roll from?"

She shrugged. "I don't know. I've never done it before.
It just felt right."

All at once, his good mood vanished as he wondered
what moves she *had* done before with other men that she
hadn't opted to try out on him. Like Liam. Was he better in
bed than his brother? Worse? About the same? And yeah,
he recognized that the burn in his gut was pure jealousy.

Totally unable to help himself, he smiled without humor
and rolled her off him casually, as if it were no big deal,
but he didn't really want her close to him right then. "It
was great. Perfect. Like you'd practiced it a lot."

What an ass he was being. But the thought of Grace

with another man, some guy's mitts on her, touching her, put him over the edge. Especially since one of those Neanderthals had been his brother.

She quirked a brow. "Really? You're not just humoring me?"

The pleased note in her voice didn't improve his mood. What, it was a compliment to be well-practiced in bed?

"Oh, no," he said silkily. "You've got the moves, sweetheart. The men must line up into the next county to get in on that."

Not only was he jealous, he was acting as if he'd been a choirboy for the past ten years when there was nothing further from the truth. He'd been the king of one-night stands because that was all he could do. It wasn't what he'd wanted or what he'd envisioned for himself, but the reason he wasn't able to move on and find someone to settle down with was sitting in his bed smiling at him as if this was all a big joke.

But as always, he wasn't going to say what was really on his mind. That was how you got hurt, by exposing your unguarded soft places.

And then she laughed. "Oh, yeah. They line up, all right. As long as we're having confession time, I have one of my own."

He needed a drink first. A row of shots would be preferable. But it was—he scowled at the clock—barely 6:00 a.m., and the babies were going to wake up any second, demanding their breakfast. "We don't have to do this, Grace."

"No, I want to," she insisted. "You told me about your leg, which was clearly hard for you. I think this is just as important for you to know. I'm not practiced. At all. It's kind of funny you'd say that actually, since you're the last man I slept with."

Shyly, she peeked at him from under lowered lashes as she let that register.

He sat up so fast, his head cracked against the head-board. "You...what?"

She hadn't been with anyone since *him*? Since ten years ago? *At all?*

Grace nodded. "I guess you could say you ruined me for other men. But that's not the only reason. I just never found one I thought measured up."

To him. She'd never found another man she'd thought was good enough. Had he been working himself up for no reason?

Grace had never been with another man. She'd been a virgin when they met. Kyle Wade was Grace's only lover. The thought choked him up in a wholly unexpected way.

And then his brain latched on to the idea of Grace refusing suitors over the years and shoved it under the lens of what he knew to be the truth. His mood turned dangerously sharp and ugly again. "Well, now. That's a high compliment. If it's true."

Confusion crept across her expression. "Why would I lie?"

"Good question. One I'd like the answer to, as well." He crossed his arms over his thundering heart. "Maybe you could explain how it's possible that you've never been with another man, yet I practically caught you in the act with one. Liam."

Just spitting his name out cost Kyle. His throat tight-ened and threatened to close off entirely, which would be great because then he couldn't throw up.

"Oh, Kyle." She actually *smiled* as she tenderly cupped his face. "You've certainly taken your time circling around back to that. Nothing happened with Liam. I didn't think you'd even noticed."

"You didn't..." He couldn't even finish that sentence and jerked away from her touch. "His hands were all over you. Don't tell me nothing happened."

"First of all, we were broken up at the time," she reminded him. "Secondly, it was a setup, honey. I wanted to get your attention, and honestly, I was pretty devastated it didn't work. Liam was a good sport about it, though. I've always appreciated that he was willing to help."

Kyle's vision went black and then red, and he squeezed his eyes shut as he came perilously close to passing out for the first time in his life. *Breathe. And again.* Ruthlessly, he got himself back under control.

"A setup," he repeated softly.

She nodded. "We set it up for you to catch us. It was dumb, I realize. Blame it on the fact that I was young and naive. I was expecting you to confront me. For us to have it out so I could explain how much you meant to me. How upset I was that we weren't together anymore. It was supposed to end differently. But you left and I figured out that I wasn't all that important to you."

A setup. To force a confrontation. And instead, she'd decided his silence meant she wasn't important to him, when in fact, the opposite was true.

"Why?" He nearly choked on the question. "Why would you do something like that? With *Liam* of all people?"

His brother. There was a sacred line between brothers that you didn't cross, and she'd not only crossed it, she'd been the instigator. Liam had put his hands on the woman Kyle loved as a *favor*. Somehow, and he wouldn't have thought this possible, that was worse than when Kyle had thought his brother was just adding another name to his growing list of conquests. The betrayal was actually twice as deep because it had all been a *setup*.

The reckoning was going to be brutal.

"Because, Kyle." She caught his gaze and tears brimmed in her eyes. "I loved you. So much and so intensely. But you were so distant. Already seeking that horizon, even then. We'd stopped connecting. Breaking up with you didn't faze you. I figured it would take something bold to shake you up."

Yeah, it had shaken him up all right. "But *that*?"

He couldn't wrap his head around what she was telling him. He'd enlisted because of a lie. Because he'd felt as though he couldn't breathe in Royal ever again. Because he'd sought a place where people stood by their word and their honor, would take a bullet for you. Where he could be part of a team alongside people who valued him. And *found* that place.

Which wasn't here.

"Yeah. Like you used Emma Jane to make me jealous." She shrugged. "Same idea. Funny how similar our tactics are."

The roaring sound in his head drowned out her words. Similar. She thought the idea of Kyle flirting with a woman out in the open in broad daylight was the same as walking by Liam's bedroom and hearing Grace's laugh. The same as peeking through the crack at the door to see the woman he'd given his soul to entwined with his brother *on his brother's bed*.

"Go." He shoved out of the bed, ignored his aching leg and dressed as fast as he could. "I can't be around you right now."

"Are you upset, Kyle?" She still sounded confused, as though it wasn't abundantly clear that none of this was okay. And then her face crumpled as understanding slowly leached into her posture.

He couldn't respond. There was nothing to say anyway.

It wasn't the same. He'd started to trust her again—no, he'd *forced* himself to forget the past despite the amount of pain he still carried around—only to find that her capacity for lies was far broader than he'd ever have imagined.

He slammed out of the room and went to make the babies' bottles because he couldn't leave as he wanted to. As he should. Grace would twist that around, too, and somehow find a way to rip his heart out again by taking his daughters away.

But he wouldn't give Grace Haines any more power in his life.

Since he couldn't leave, Kyle stewed. When Liam and Hadley returned from Vail the next afternoon, Kyle wasn't fit company.

Which made it the perfect time for a confrontation.

"Liam," Kyle fairly growled as he cornered his brother in the kitchen after Hadley went to the nursery to see the babies.

"What's up?" Liam chugged some water from the bottle in his hand.

"Grace fessed up." Crossing his arms so he wouldn't get started on the beating portion of the reckoning too soon, he shifted the weight off his bad leg and glared at the betrayer who dared stand there scowling as though he didn't know what Kyle was talking about. "Back before I went into the navy. You and Grace. It was a lie."

"Oh, that." Liam shook his head. "Yeah, you're a little slow on the uptake. That's ancient history."

"It's recent to me because I just found out about it."

With a smirk, Liam punched him on the arm. "Maybe if you'd stuck around instead of flying off to the navy, you'd have known then. That was the whole purpose of it, according to Grace, to get you to confront her. I was just window dressing."

"I went into the navy because of window dressing," Kyle said through clenched teeth, though how his brain was still functioning enough to spit out thoughts was beyond him. "Glad to know this is all a big game to everyone. I've been missing out. Where's Hadley? I'm looking forward to getting in on some of this fun. Would you like to watch while I feel up your wife or would you rather walk in on us?"

"Shut your filthy mouth."

Kyle was ready for his brother this time and blocked Liam's crappy right hook easily, pushing back on his twin's torso before the man charged him. "Not so fun when you're on the other side of it, huh?"

Chest heaving and eyes wild with fury, Liam strained against Kyle's immovable blockade. "What do you care? You ignored Grace to the point where she cried so much over your sorry hide, I thought she was going to dry up like an old withered flower."

"Aren't you the poet?" He sneered to cover the catch in his heart to hear that Grace had cried over him. And how did Liam know that anyway? It probably wasn't even true. This was all an elaborate bunch of hooey designed to throw Kyle off the scent of who was really to blame here. "I cared, you idiot. You're the one who didn't care about the big fat line you crossed when you put your hands on my woman."

"*Your* woman? I got a feeling Grace would disagree." Liam snorted and stepped back, mercifully, allowing Kyle to drop his hand from his brother's chest. Another few minutes of holding him back would have strained his leg something fierce. "What line did I cross? You broke up. You weren't even together when that happened, remember?"

"*She* broke up. I didn't," Kyle countered viciously. "I was trying to figure out how to get her back. Not so easy when a woman tells you she's through and then makes out with another guy. Who happens to be my brother. Which never would have happened if you'd told her no. *That's* the line, Liam. I would never have done that to you."

Something dawned in Liam's gaze. "Holy cow. You were in love with her."

"What the hell do you think I've been talking about?"

Disgusted with the circles and lies and betrayals, Kyle slumped against the counter, seriously thinking about starting on a bottle of Irish whiskey. It was five o'clock 24-7 when you found out your twin brother was a complete moron.

"You were in love with her," Liam repeated with surprise, as if saying it again was going to make it more real. "Still are."

Well, *duh*. Of course he was! Why did Liam think Kyle was so pissed?

Wait. No, that wasn't— Kyle shut his eyes for a beat, but the truth didn't magically become something else. Of course he was still in love with Grace. That's why her betrayal hurt so much.

"That's not the point." Nor was that up for discussion. It didn't matter anyway. He and Grace were through, for real this time.

"No, the point is that this is all news to me. Probably news to Grace as well, assuming you actually got around to telling her." More comprehension dawned in Liam's expression. "You haven't. You're still just as much of a jackass now as you were then."

Kyle was getting really tired of being so transparent. "Some things shouldn't have to be said."

Liam laughed so hard, Kyle thought he was going to bust something, and the longer it went on, the more Kyle wanted to be the one doing the busting. Like a couple of teeth in his brother's mouth.

Finally, Liam wiped his eyes. "Get your checkbook because you need to buy a clue, my brother. No woman is going to let you get away with being such a clam, so keep on being the strong, silent type and sleep alone. See if I care."

"Yeah, you're the fount of wisdom when it comes to women, Mr. Revolving Door. Do you even know how many women you've slept with over the years?" Cheap shot. And Kyle knew it the moment it left his mouth, but Liam had him good and riled. He started to apologize but Liam waved it off.

"That doesn't matter when you find the right one." Liam glanced up the back stairs fondly, his mind clearly on his wife, who was still upstairs with the babies. "But guess what? You don't get a woman like Hadley without knowing a few things about how to treat a woman. And keeping your thoughts to yourself ain't it. Look what it's cost you so far. You willing to spend the next ten years without the woman you love because of your man-of-few-words shtick?"

Yeah, he didn't blather on about the stuff that was inside. So what? It was personal and he didn't like to share it.

Keeping quiet was a defense mechanism he'd adopted when he was little to shelter him from constantly being in a place he didn't fit into, lest anyone figure out his real feelings. Some wounds weren't obvious but they went deep.

The old-fashioned clock on the wall ticked out the seconds as it had done since Kyle was old enough to know how to tell time. Back then, he'd marked each one on his heart, counting the ticks in hopes that when he reached a thousand, his mother would come back. When he reached ten thousand, she'd *surely* walk through the door. A hundred thousand. And then he'd lose count and start over.

She had never come back to rescue him from the ranch he didn't like, didn't comprehend. Nothing had ever fit right until Grace. She was still the only woman who ever had.

And maybe he'd messed up a little by not telling her what she meant to him. Okay, maybe he'd messed up a lot. If he'd told her, she probably wouldn't have cooked up that scheme with Liam. Too little, too late.

"We good?" Liam asked, his gaze a lot more understanding than it should have been.

"Yeah." Kyle sighed. "It was a long time ago."

"For what it's worth, I'm sorry."

Liam stuck his hand out and Kyle didn't hesitate. They shook on it and did an awkward one-armed brotherly hug that probably looked more like two squirrels fighting over a walnut than anything. But it was enough to bury the hatchet, and not in Liam's back, the way Kyle had planned when he'd stormed into the kitchen earlier.

"Listen." Liam cleared his throat. "If we're all done crying about your girlfriend, I've got something to tell you that's been rubbing me the wrong way."

"You need me to go underwear shopping with you so we can get you the right size?" When Liam elbowed him, Kyle knew they were on the way back to being brothers again instead of strangers. "Because you have a wife for that now."

"Shut up. This is for serious. There's an outfit called Samson Oil making noises around Royal and I don't like it. They're buying up properties. Even offered me a pretty penny for Wade Ranch. Wanted to make sure you're on the same—"

"You said no, right?" Kyle shot back instantly. This was his home now. The place he planned to raise his daughters. No amount of money could compensate for a stable home life for his family.

"Well, I wanted to talk to you first. But yeah. The right answer is no."

Relief squeezed his chest. And wasn't that something? Kyle had never thought he'd consider the ranch home. But there you go. The threat of losing it—well, he didn't have to worry about that, obviously.

"So it's a no. What's the big deal then?"

Liam shrugged. "I dunno. It just doesn't sit well. The

guy from Sampson, he didn't even look around. Just handed me some paperwork with an offer that was fifteen million above fair market value. How's that for a big deal?"

It ruffled the back of Kyle's neck, too. "There's no oil around here. What little there is has a pump on it already."

"Yeah, so now you're where I'm at. It's weird, right?"

Kyle nodded because his throat was tight again. It was nice to be consulted. As if he really was half owner of the ranch, and he and Liam were going to do this thing called family. He hadn't left this time and it might have made a huge difference.

It gave Kyle hope he might actually become the father his girls deserved. Grace, however, was a whole other story with an ending he couldn't quite figure out.

Ten

Grace kicked the oven. It didn't magically turn on. It hadn't the first time she'd hauled off and whacked it a minute ago, either.

But kicking something felt good. Her foot throbbed, which was better than the numbness she'd felt since climbing from Kyle's bed, well loved and then brokenhearted in the space of an hour. The physical pain was a far sight better than the mental pain.

Because she didn't understand what had happened. She'd opened her heart to Kyle again, only to be destroyed more thoroughly the second time than she had been the first time. This was a grown woman's pain. And the difference was breathtaking. Literally, as in she couldn't make her lungs expand enough to get a good, solid full breath.

Determined to fix something, Grace spent twenty minutes unscrewing every bolt she could budge on the oven, hoping something would jump out at her as the culprit. Which failed miserably because she didn't know what it was supposed to look like—how would she know if something was out of place? The oven was just broken. No matter. She wasn't hungry anyway.

She wandered around her small house two blocks off the main street of Royal. She'd bought the house three years ago when she'd claimed her Professional Single Girl status, and set about finding a way to be happy with the idea of building a life with herself and herself only in it. She had, to a degree. No one argued with her if she wanted to change the drapes four times a year, and she never had to share the bathroom.

The empty rooms hadn't seemed so empty until now. Spending the weekend with Kyle had stomped her fantasy of being single and happy to pieces. She wanted a husband to fill the space in her bed, in her heart. Children who laughed around the kitchen table. A dog the kids named something silly, like Princess Spaghetti.

A fierce knock sounded at the door, echoing through the whole house. She almost didn't answer it because who else would knock like that except a man who had a lot of built-up anger? At her, apparently. After ten years of turning over every aspect of her relationship with Kyle, analyzing it to death while looking for the slightest nuance of where it had all gone wrong, never once had she turned that inspection back on herself.

But she'd made mistakes, that much was apparent. Then and now. Somehow.

Only she didn't quite buy that what happened ten years ago was all her fault.

And all at once, she wanted that reckoning. Wanted to ask a few pointed questions of Kyle Wade that she hadn't gotten to ask before being thrown out of his bed two long and miserable days ago.

She yanked open the door and the mad she'd worked up faltered.

Kyle stood there on her doorstep in crisp jeans, boots and a work shirt, dressed like every other man in Royal and probably a hundred other towns dotting the Texas prairie. But he wasn't anything close to any other man the world over, because he was Kyle. Her stupid heart would probably never get the message that they were doomed as a couple.

He was holding a bouquet of beautiful flowers, so full it spilled over his hand in a riot of colors and shapes. Her vision blurred as she focused on the flowers and the solemn expression on Kyle's face.

"Hey, Grace."

No. He wasn't allowed to be here all apologetic and carrying conciliatory flowers. It wasn't fair. She couldn't let him into her head again, and she certainly wasn't offering up her heart again to be flattened. He didn't have to know she'd given up on getting over him.

"What do you want, Kyle?" She didn't even wince at her own rudeness. She got a pass after being shown the door while still undressed and warm from the man's arms.

"I brought you these," he said simply without blinking at her harsh tone. He held out the bouquet. "Thank-you flowers. Because I owed you."

Wasn't *that* romantic? She didn't take the bouquet. "You *owed* me? You definitely owe me, but not flowers. An explanation would be better."

Kyle dropped the bouquet, his expression hardening. "May I come in then? Your next-door neighbor is out on the porch with popcorn, watching the show."

"Mrs. Putter is seventy-two." Grace crossed her arms and propped a hip against the doorjamb. "This is all the fun she gets for the year."

"Fine." Kyle sighed. "I came to apologize. I shot first and asked questions later. It's the way I do things, mostly because people are usually shooting at me, too."

Not an auspicious start, other than the apology part. "And yet I still haven't heard any questions."

"Grace." Kyle caught her gaze, and something warm spilled from his green eyes that she couldn't look away from. "You meant something to me. Back then. You have to understand that I had a lot of stuff going on in my head that I didn't want to deal with, so I didn't. I shut down instead. That wasn't fair to you. But you were the best thing in my life, and then you were gone. I was a wreck. Seeing you with Liam was the last straw, so I left Royal because I couldn't stand it, assuming that you'd found the Wade brother you preferred. There was never a point when I would have confronted you about it."

Openmouthed, she stared at him. That was the longest speech she'd ever heard him give and it loosened her tongue in kind. "I get that I messed up with Liam. I was young and stupid. I should have been more up-front about my feelings, too."

Kyle nodded. "Goes for both of us. But I still owe you a thank-you. I joined the military because I wanted to be gone. I figured, what better way to forget Royal and the girl there than to go to the other side of the world in defense of my country? But instead of just a place to nurse my shattered ego, I found something I didn't expect. Something great. Being a SEAL changed me."

Yes, she'd seen that. He'd grown up, into a responsible, solid man who cared about his daughters. "You seem to have flourished."

"I did," he agreed enthusiastically. "It was the team I'd been looking for. I never fit in at the ranch. That's part of what was weighing me down back then. The stuff inside. I was contemplating my future and not seeing a clear picture of what I should do going forward. If you hadn't staged that ploy with Liam, I might never have found my unit. Those guys were my family."

The sheer emotion on his face as he talked about his fellow team members—it was overwhelming. He'd clearly loved being in the military. It had shaped him, and he'd soaked it up.

Her heart twisted anew. If he didn't fit in at the ranch, why had he taken over the cattle side? During one of her site visits, he'd told her that was his job now—he hoped to create a stable home for his daughters. He planned to stick around this time. Was that all a lie? Or was he just doing it because she'd forced him into it, despite hating that life?

"I don't understand," she whispered. "If you liked being in the military so much, why did you come home?"

"My leg." His expression caved in on itself, and it might have been the most vulnerable she'd ever seen him. She almost reached out to comfort him, was almost physically unable to prevent her heart from crying in sympathy at what he'd lost. He was hurting, and that was so hard for her to take.

But she didn't reach out. "You came home because you were injured," she recounted flatly.

That was the only reason. Not because he missed Grace and regretted splitting up. Not because he wanted his daughters, or the simple life on a ranch with his family. He'd been forced to.

And what would he do when he got tired of an ill-fitting career? What would happen when the allure of the great wide open called to him again?

He'd leave. Just as he'd done the first time, only he'd take his babies with him—there was no law that said he had to stay in Royal to retain custody. He'd go and crush her anew, once she'd fallen in love with three people instead of just one.

He hadn't confronted her about Liam ten years ago because he hadn't wanted to stay in the first place. Not for her, not for anything. If he had, he'd have fought for their love; she had no doubt.

Kyle could pretend all he wanted that he'd enlisted because he'd caught her with Liam, but that had been—by his own admission—the last straw. Not the first.

"Yeah." He jerked his head in acknowledgment. "I was honorably discharged due to my busted leg. I didn't have anyplace else to go. But when I saw Maddie and Maggie for the first time…and then you came back into my life… Well, things are different now. I want to do things different. Starting with you."

"No." Her heart nearly split in two as she shook her head. "We've already had one too many do-overs. You shot first and asked questions too late."

She'd begun to trust him again, only to have the carpet ripped out from under her feet. She couldn't do that again. She could be single and happy. It was a choice; she just had to make it.

"Don't say that, Grace." Kyle threw the bouquet on the wicker chair closest to the door and captured her hand, squeezing it tight so she couldn't pull away. His green eyes beseeched her to reconsider, hollowing her out inside. "I lie awake at night and think about how great it would be if you were there. I think about what it's going to be like for the girls growing up without a mom. It's not a picture I like. We need someone to keep us sane."

This was delivered with a lopsided smile that she ached to return. If only he'd mentioned the condition of his heart in that speech and how it was breaking to be away from her. How he couldn't consider his life complete without her. Anything other than a string of sentences which sounded suspiciously like an invitation to make sure Maddie and Maggie had a mother figure.

And she wanted a family so badly she could picture easily falling into the role of Mama to those precious babies. At what cost, though?

"You have Hadley for that," she said woodenly. "I'm unnecessary."

"You're not listening to what I'm saying." He held her hand against his chest, and she wanted to uncurl her palm so she could feel his heartbeat. "Hadley is Liam's wife. I want one of my own."

It was the closest thing to a proposal she'd ever gotten. She was certifiably insane for not saying yes. Except he hadn't actually asked her. As always, he couldn't just come right out and say what he meant. That's what had led to the Liam fiasco in the first place, and nothing had changed.

None of this was what she'd envisioned. Kyle was nothing like her father. What about her standards? Her grand romance and fairy-tale life? How in the world would their relationship ever stand the test of time with staged jealousy-inducing ploys and the inability to just talk to each other as their starting point?

"I can't do this, Kyle. I can't—" Her voice broke but she made herself finish. "I thought we were starting something and the moment things get a little rough, you bail. Just like before."

"That's an excuse, Grace." He firmed his mouth, and then pointed out, "I'm here now, aren't I?"

"It's too late," she retorted, desperate to get this horrific conversation over with. "We have too many trust issues. We don't even want the same things."

His green eyes sharpened as he absorbed her words. "How can you say that? I want to be together. That's the same."

"Except that's not what I want," she whispered, and forced herself to watch as his beautiful face blanked, becoming as desolate as a West Texas ravine in a drought. "Goodbye, Kyle."

And before she took it all back in a moment of weakness, she shut the door, dry-eyed. The tears would come later.

Now that Johnny and Slim had a grudging respect for Kyle as the boss, they got on okay.

Which was fortunate, because Kyle drove them all relentlessly. Himself included, and probably the hardest. Spring calving season was in full swing and eighteen-hour days fit with Kyle's determination to never think, never lie awake at night and never miss Grace.

At this point, he'd take two out of three, but the hole where Grace was supposed to be ached too badly to be ignored, which in turn guaranteed he wouldn't sleep. And as he lay there not sleeping, his brain did nothing but think, turning over her words again and again, forcing him to relive them because he deserved to be unhappy. He couldn't be with Grace because she didn't want to be with him. Because she didn't trust him.

All the work he'd done to get over his trust issues, and she'd blindsided him with her own. Because he'd left when life got too difficult. When all he'd wanted was to find his place in the world. And when that place spat him back out, he came back. To forge a new place, put down roots. It had been hard, one of the toughest challenges of his life, and yeah, when it got rough, he dreamed of leaving. But he hadn't. Only to have that thrown back in his face.

If it didn't hurt so bad he'd laugh at the irony.

A week after Operation: Grace had gone down in flames, Liam invited him to the Texas Cattlemen's Club for an afternoon of "getting away from it all" as Liam put it. Curious about the club his grandfather had belonged to, and now Liam, too, apparently, Kyle agreed, with the caveat that they'd only stay a couple of hours tops. The cattle weren't going to tend themselves, after all.

The moment Kyle walked into the formerly men-only club, the outside world ceased to exist. Dark hardwood floors stretched from wall to wall, reflecting the pale gold wallpaper that warmed the place. It was welcoming and hushed, as if the room was waiting for something important to happen. The sense of anticipation was compelling.

Kyle followed Liam to the bar, where some other men sat nursing beers. Kyle recognized Mac McCallum, who'd been Liam's buddy for a long time, and Case Baxter.

"Case is the president of the Texas Cattlemen's Club," Liam said as he introduced everyone around. "And this is Nolan Dane."

"Right." Kyle shook the man's hand. "Haven't seen you in ages."

"I'm back in town, practicing family law now," Nolan explained with a glance at Liam. "Your brother's a client."

Kyle nodded as his lungs hitched. Liam had a legal retainer who practiced family law? Didn't take a rocket scientist to do that math. When Liam had talked about papers and warned Kyle he'd need a lawyer, it hadn't been an idle threat. They hadn't talked about it again, and Kyle had hoped the idea of adoption had been dropped.

Obviously it hadn't.

But why stick it in Kyle's face like this? It was a crappy thing to do after all the hoops Kyle'd been forced to jump through to prove his worth as a father. *Especially* after they'd had their Come To Jesus discussion and Liam had apologized for the Grace thing.

Wasn't that indicative of Kyle's Royal welcome thus far? That's why he shot first. When he didn't, he invariably took a bullet straight into his gut.

Mouth firmly shut as he processed everything, Kyle took a seat as far away from Liam as he could. When the conversation turned to Samson Oil, it piqued his interest sufficiently to pull his head out of his rear long enough to participate. Especially when Nolan Dane excused himself with a pained look on his face.

"More offers for land coming in," Liam affirmed. "Wade Ranch included. I think we've got a problem on our hands."

The other men seemed to share his brother's concern. Kyle leaned in. "What does Samson Oil want? They have to know the oil prospects are slim to none around here. People been drilling for over a hundred years. There's no way Samson will find a new well."

Case Baxter shook his head. "No one knows for sure what they're up to. Fracking, maybe. But the Cline Shale property is mostly bought up already in this area."

"If you've got concerns, I've got concerns," Kyle said as his senses tingled again. "I know a guy in the CIA. Owes me a favor. I'll have him poke around, see what Samson Oil is up to."

The offer was out of his mouth before he'd thought better of it. He didn't owe these people anything. It wasn't as if they'd rolled out the red carpet for the returning war veteran. Or acknowledged that Kyle Wade owned half a *cattle ranch* and wasn't even a member of the Texas Cattleman's Club.

Royal clearly wasn't where Kyle fit, any more than he had ten years ago.

"I knew you'd come in handy." Liam fairly beamed.

"That would be great," Mac threw in. "The more information we have, the better. The last thing we need is to find out they're looking for a site to house a new strip mall after it's too late."

The expectant faces of the men surrounding him settled Kyle's resolve. He couldn't take it back now. And for better or worse, this was his home, and he had a responsibility to it. He shrugged.

"Consider it done." Kyle sat back and let the members

of the club do their thing, which didn't include him. If he kept his mouth shut, maybe everyone would forget about him. It wasn't as if he wanted to be a member of their exclusive club anyway.

But then Liam's phone beeped, and he glanced at it, frowning. When his grave and troubled gaze met Kyle's, every nerve in Kyle's body stood on end.

"We have to go," Liam announced. "Sorry."

Liam hustled Kyle out of the club and into his truck, ignoring Kyle's rapid-fire questions about the nature of the emergency. Because of course there was one. Liam's face only looked like that when something bad happened to one of his prized horses.

Liam started the truck and tore out of the lot before finally finding his voice. "It's Maddie."

All the blood drained from Kyle's head and his chest squeezed so tight, it was a wonder his heart didn't push through two ribs. "What? What do you mean, it's Maddie? What happened?"

Not a horse. His daughter. Maddie.

"Hadley's not sure," Liam hedged. Kyle gripped his forearm, growling. "Driving here. Causing me to have a wreck won't get you the information any faster. I'm taking you to Royal Memorial. Hadley said Maddie wouldn't wake up and had a really high fever. With Maddie's heart problems, that's a really bad sign because she might have an infection. Hadley called an ambulance and left Maggie in Candace's capable hands. We're meeting them there."

The drive couldn't have taken more than five minutes. But it took five years off Kyle's life to be trapped in the cab of Liam's truck when his poor defenseless Maddie was suffering. The baby was fragile, and while she'd been growing steadily, obviously her insides weren't as strong as they should be. His mind leaped ahead to all the ugly possibilities, and he wished his heart *had* fallen out earlier, because the thought of losing one of his daughters—it was far worse than losing Grace. Worse than losing his place on his SEAL team.

Liam screeched into the lot, but Kyle had the door open before he'd fully rolled to a stop, hitting the pavement at a run. It was a much different technique from jumping out of a plane, and his leg hadn't been busted on his last HALO mission.

Pain knifed up his knee and clear into his chest cavity, which didn't need any more stress. The leg nearly crumpled underneath him, but he ignored it and stormed into the emergency room, looking for a doctor to unleash his anxiety on.

The waiting room receptionist met him halfway across the room. "Mr. Wade. Hadley requested that you be brought to the pediatric ICU immediately. Follow me."

ICU? Shades of the tiny room in Germany where Kyle had lain in a stupor for months filtered back through his consciousness, and his stomach rolled involuntarily, threatening to expel the beer he'd been happily drinking while his daughter was being subjected to any number of frightening people and procedures. The elevator dinged but he barely registered it above the numbness. Liam and the receptionist flanked him, both poor wingmen in a dire situation. But all he had.

Finally, they emerged onto the second floor and set off down the hall. Hadley rushed into Liam's arms, tears streaming down her face. They murmured to each other, but Kyle skirted them, seeking his little pink bundle, to assure himself she was okay and Maggie wouldn't have to grow up without her sister. The girls had already been through so much, so many hits that Kyle had already missed.

But he was here now. Ready to fight back against whatever was threatening his family. And that included his brother. The adoption business needed to be put to rest. Immediately.

"Who's in charge around here?" Kyle growled at the receptionist, who must have been used to people in crisis because she just smiled.

"I'll find the nurse to speak to you. Dr. Reese is in with your daughter now."

The receptionist disappeared into the maze of hospital rooms and corridors.

Hadley and Liam came up on either side of Kyle, and Hadley placed a comforting hand on his arm. "Dr. Reese is the best. He's been caring for Maddie since she was born. He'll know what to do."

That was far from comforting. If only he could see her, he'd feel a lot better.

A woman in scrubs with balloon decals all over them emerged from a room and walked straight to Kyle. "Hi, Mr. Wade, I'm Clare Connolly, if you don't remember me. We've got Maddie on an IV and a ventilator. She's stable and that's the important thing."

"What happened? What's wrong with her?" Kyle demanded.

"Dr. Reese is concerned about the effects of her high fever on her heart," Clare said frankly, which Kyle appreciated. "He's trying to bring the fever down and running some tests to see what's happening. The last surgery should have fixed all the problems, but nothing is guaranteed. We knew that going in and, well, we're going to keep fighting. We all want to win this thing once and for all."

This woman genuinely cared about Maddie. He could see it in the worried set of her mouth. Nurses were never emotional about their patients, or at least the German ones weren't.

"Thanks. For everything you're doing. May I talk to the doctor?"

"Of course. He'll want to talk to you, too. We all want to see Maddie running alongside her sister and blowing out candles on her birthday cakes for a long time to come. When Dr. Reese is free, he'll be out," Clare promised, and extended her hand toward the waiting room outside the pediatric unit. "Why don't you have a seat until then."

Clare bustled back into the room she'd materialized from, and Kyle nearly followed her because the waiting room was for people who had the capacity to wait, and that did not describe Kyle.

But Hadley's hand on his arm stopped him. "Let the doctor do his thing, Kyle. You'll only be in the way."

Long minutes stretched as Kyle hovered outside his daughter's room. What was taking so long? Pacing didn't help. It hurt. Everything inside hurt. Finally, another nurse dared approach him, explaining that the hall needed to be clear in case of emergency. Wouldn't he please take a seat?

He did, for no other reason than it would be a relief to get off his leg. Now if only he could find something to do with his hands.

People began filtering into the waiting room. Mac McCallum came to sit with Liam and Hadley, who promptly excused herself to fill out paperwork for Maddie, which she'd offered to do in Kyle's stead so he could be available the moment the doctor came out with news. Hadley's friend Kori came in and took a seat next to Liam.

They all had smiles and words of encouragement for Kyle. Some had stories of how Maddie was a fighter and how many people had sat with her through the night when she was known as Baby Janey. This community had embraced his daughter before they'd even known whom she belonged to. And now that they did, nothing had changed. They still cared. They were all here to provide support during a crisis, which is what the very best of neighbors did.

And then the air shifted, prickling Kyle's skin. He looked up.

Grace.

She rushed into the room, brown curls flying, and knelt by his chair, bringing the scent of spring and innocence and everything good in the world along with her. As he soaked up her presence, he took his first easy breath since Hadley's message to Liam had upended his insides.

"I came as soon as Hadley called me," she said, her brown eyes huge and distressed as her gaze flitted over him.

The muffled hospital noises and people and everything around them faded as they focused on each other. Greedily, he searched her beautiful face for some hint as to her thoughts. Was she getting any sleep? Did she miss him?

She slid her hand into his and held on. "I'm sorry about Maddie. How are you doing?"

"Okay," he said gruffly.

Better now. Much better. How was it possible that the woman who continually ripped his heart out could repair it instantly just by walking into a room?

It was a paradox he didn't understand.

She climbed into the next chair, her grip on his hand never lessening. Her skin warmed his, and it was only then that he realized how cold he'd been.

"What did Dr. Reese say?" she asked.

Did everyone in town know the name of his daughter's pediatrician? "He hasn't been out yet. The nurse, Ms. Connelly, said her fever might be causing problems with her heart, but we don't know anything for sure."

His voice broke then, as sheer overwhelming helplessness swamped him, weighing down his arms and legs when all he wanted to do was explode from this chair and go pound on someone until they fixed his precious little bundle of pink.

"Oh, no." Grace's free hand flew to her mouth in anguish. "That's the one thing we were hoping wouldn't happen."

He nodded, swallowing rapidly so he could speak.

"Thanks," he said. "For coming."

He wouldn't have called her. But now that she was here Grace was exactly what he'd needed, and he never would have taken steps to make it happen. What if she'd said no? But she hadn't, and he didn't care about anything other than sitting here waiting on news about his daughter with the woman he loved. Still. In spite of everything.

If only it made a difference.

Eleven

Grace normally loved being at Royal Memorial because 99 percent of the time, she was there because someone was giving birth. That was a joyous event worthy of celebration. Waiting on news about the health and well-being of Kyle's baby was hands down one of the most stressful things she'd ever done.

At the same time, it was turning into a community event, the kind that strengthened ties and bonded people together. And she hadn't let go of Kyle's hand once. People seemed unsurprised to see them together. Not that they were "together." But they were easy with each other in a way that probably looked natural to others.

Inside, she was a bit of a mess.

How many times had she replayed that last conversation with Kyle in her head, wondering if she'd been too harsh, too unforgiving? If her standards were too high? She'd finally had to shut it down, telling herself ten times a day that she'd stood up for what she wanted for a reason. Kyle wasn't a safe bet for her heart. He'd proven that over and over.

But being here with him in his time of need brought all the questions back in a rush. Because it didn't feel as if they were through. It felt as if they were exactly where they were supposed to be—together.

It was all very confusing. She just hoped that supporting him during this crisis didn't give him the wrong idea—that she might be willing to forget her standards. Forget that he'd stomped on her heart again the moment she'd let her guard down.

Grace had lost track of the hour and only glanced at the clock when Kyle's stomach grumbled. Just as she was about to offer to get him something to eat, Dr. Reese appeared at the entrance to the waiting room, looking worn but smiling.

The entire room ceased to talk. Move. Breathe.

She and Kyle both tightened their grip on each other's hands simultaneously. When he rose, she followed him to the edge of the waiting room, where Dr. Reese was waiting to talk to Kyle privately. She stepped closer to Kyle in silent support, just in case the news wasn't as good as the expression on Dr. Reese's face might indicate.

"I'm Dr. Reese." Parker held out his hand for Kyle to shake. "Your daughter is stable. I was able to bring the fever down, which is a good sign, but I don't know if it adversely affected her heart yet. I need to keep her overnight for observation and run some more tests in the morning after we've both had some sleep. She's a fighter, and I have high hopes that this is only a minor setback with no long-term effects. But I'll know more in the morning."

"Call me Kyle. Formality is for strangers," Kyle said, and his relieved exhale mirrored Grace's. "And any man who saved Maddie's life is a friend of mine. Can I see her?"

Parker nodded instantly. "Sure, of course. She's asleep

right now, but there's no reason you can't stay with her, if you want—"

"Yes," Kyle broke in fiercely. "I'll be there until you kick me out."

That meant Grace wasn't going anywhere, either. If there were rules about that sort of thing, someone could complain to the hospital board, the mayor and Sheriff Battle. Tomorrow. No one was going to stand between her and the man who needed her.

Unless Kyle didn't want her there.

Would be weird to spend the night in the hospital with a man she'd told to get lost?

But then he turned to her, his expression flickering between cautious optimism and fatigue. "I'm glad you're here."

And that decided it. It still might be weird for her to stay, but he needed her, and she could no sooner ignore that than she could magically fix Maddie's frightening health problems.

They gave the others a rundown of the situation and implored them to spend the night in comfort at their homes with a promise to call or text everyone with more news in the morning. With hugs and more murmured encouragement, one by one, the full waiting room emptied out. Kyle smiled, shaking hands and accepting hugs from the women, while Grace watched him out of the corner of her eye to ensure he was doing okay.

What she saw surprised her. His small smile for each person was genuine and he returned hugs easily. For someone who hadn't wanted to come home, he'd meshed into the community well enough. Did he realize it?

Hadley stayed where she was.

"Liam and I will wait with you," she insisted, stubbornly crossing her arms.

Liam quickly hustled Hadley to her feet with a hushed

word in her ear. Whatever he said made her uncross her arms but didn't get her moving out of the waiting room any faster.

"I appreciate that," Kyle said. "But it's not necessary. You've done enough. Besides, I need someone I trust at home with Maggie, so Candace can get back to her house-keeping. That's the most important thing you can do for me."

Grace's heart twisted as she got more confirmation that she'd made the right decision in leaving Maddie and Maggie with Kyle—he clearly had both his daughters' interests in the forefront of his mind.

"Candace is trustworthy," Hadley countered. "She's watched Maggie plenty of times."

Liam captured his wife's hand and pulled on it, his exaggerated expression almost comical. "Sweetie, *Grace* is staying with Kyle."

Comprehension slowly leached into her gaze as Hadley finally caught her husband's drift. She started shuffling toward the exit. "Well, if you're sure. We'll be a phone call away."

And then they were gone, leaving Grace alone with Kyle. There was still tension between them but for now, the focus was on Maddie. This was the part where they'd be adults about their issues, just as they should have been all along, and get through the night.

"Guess they thought they'd leave us to our romantic evening," Kyle commented wryly as he nodded after Hadley and Liam. "I'm pretty sure that's why they went to Vail. To give me the house to myself for the weekend in hopes that I'd call you."

Not to get him to step up for his girls. That wasn't even necessary, probably hadn't been from the beginning. Liam and Hadley had gone to Vail for *her* benefit. Hers and Kyle's. And it would have been perfect if she and Kyle had only hashed out their issues before getting involved again, instead of hiding behind their defense mechanisms.

That's why she couldn't give him the slightest false hope that she was here because she wanted to try again. The problem was that she might have given *herself* that false hope.

For all her conviction that she'd made the right decision to walk away from him, something inside kept whispering that maybe it wasn't too late to take a step toward talking about their issues.

"Will you go with me to see Maddie?" Kyle's eyes blinked closed for a moment. "I'm not sure I can go in there by myself."

He'd been stalling. How had she missed that? Because she was busy worrying about what was going on with the state of their relationship instead of worrying about the reason they were here: Maddie. Some support system she was.

Grace smiled as she took his hand again, holding tight. "I'm here. For as long as you need me."

When his eyes opened, he caught her up in that diamond-hard green gaze of his. "Grace," he murmured, "come sit with me."

Meekly, she complied, following him into the hospital room where Maddie lay asleep in a bed with a railing. It looked so much like her crib at home, but so vastly wrong. Machines surrounded her, hooked to wires and tubes that were attached to her tender skin. Grace almost couldn't stand to internalize it.

Clare was checking something on one of the machines and smiled as they came in. "She's doing okay. Worn out from the tests. That couch against the window lies flat, like a futon, if you plan to stay. I have to check on some other patients but we've got Maddie on top-notch monitors, and I'll be back in a couple of hours. Press this button if you notice any change or need anything."

She held up a plastic wand with a red button at the end. Kyle nodded. "Thanks. We'll be fine."

Then Clare bustled out of the room, leaving them alone with Maddie.

"I would trade places with her in a New York minute," Kyle said softly, his gaze on his daughter. "I would *pay* if someone would let me trade places. She's so fragile and tiny. How is her body holding up under all of those things poked into her? It's not right."

Grace nodded, her throat so raw from holding back tears, she wasn't sure she could speak.

All at once, he spun toward her, catching her up in his desperate embrace, burying his head in her hair. She clung to him as his chest shuddered against hers while they both struggled to get their anguish under control.

"I'm sorry," she whispered, forcing the words out.

"Thank you for staying with me. My life was so empty, Grace," he murmured. "For so long, I was a part of something, and then I wasn't."

"I know." She nodded. "You told me how much the military meant to you."

"*No*. Not that. *You*." Fiercely, he clasped her face in both palms and lifted her head and spoke directly to her soul. "Grace. Please. We have to find a way to make it work this time because I can't do this without you. I need you. I love you. I always have."

And then he was kissing her, pouring a hundred different meanings into it. Longing. Distress. Passion. Fear.

She kissed him back, because *yes*, she felt those things, too. He was telling her what she meant to him, first verbally and then through their kiss, and she was finally listening. But this was how it was with them. She got her hopes up and he dashed them.

What could possibly be different this time? She took

the kiss down a notch, and then pulled back. "Sit down with me and let's talk. For once."

That was *not* what she'd meant to say. She should have said no. Told him flat out that they were not happening again. But the eagerness on his face at her suggestion—maybe talking was that start toward something different than what she'd been looking for.

"We're not so good at the talking, are we?" he asked rhetorically, and let her lead him to the couch. They settled in together and held hands as they watched the monitors beep and shush for a moment. "I'm sorry about Emma Jane."

That was so out of the blue, she glanced at him sideways. "I've already forgotten that."

"I haven't. It was low. And totally unfair to both of you. I apologized to her, too." He stared at Maddie, his gaze uneasy. "I wish I had a better excuse for why I did it. I have a hard time just coming out and saying what's going on with me."

She bit her tongue—hard—to keep from blurting out, *Hallelujah and amen.* She didn't say a word. Barely.

"It doesn't come naturally," he continued, his voice strained, and her heart ached a little as he struggled to form his thoughts. "I'm used to being stomped on by people I trust, and I guess I have a tendency to keep my mouth shut. My rationale is that if I don't tell people what I'm feeling, I don't get hurt."

The tears that had been threatening spilled over then, sliding down her face as she heard the agony in his words. He fell silent for a moment, and she started to give him a pass on whatever else he was about to say, but he glanced at her and used his thumb to wipe the trail of tears from her cheek.

His lips lifted in a wry smile. "Guess what? It doesn't work."

Vehemently, she shook her head, more tears flying. "No,

it doesn't. If I'd just told you how I was feeling ten years ago instead of breaking up with you and then pulling that ridiculous stunt with Liam, we'd be at a different place. Instead, I hurt both of us for no reason."

All of that had been born out of her own inability to tell him what was going on with *her*. They were so alike, it was frightening. How had she never realized that?

"I've already forgotten that," he said, and this time, his smile was genuine and full.

"I haven't," she shot back sarcastically in a parody of their earlier conversation. "I spent ten years trying to forget you, and guess what? It doesn't work."

"For the record, I forgave you way before I ever showed up at your door with those poor flowers."

Chagrin heated her cheeks. That was mercy she didn't deserve. Actually, none of this was what she deserved—which would be for Kyle to walk out of this room with his daughter and never speak to her again.

Instead, it looked as though they were on the verge of a real second chance. *Please, God. Let that be true.*

"I'm sorry about the flowers. I was just so hurt and mad. It never even occurred to me that part of the problem was that I wasn't opening my mouth any more than you were. I don't even have a good excuse. So I'm trying to do things differently this time. Starting now." She covered their joined hands with her other one, aching to touch him, to increase the contact just a bit. "I have a hard time with separating what I think something should look like from reality. I wanted you to be dashing and romantic. Sweep me off my feet with over-the-top gestures and babble on with pretty poetry about how I was your sun and moon. Silly stuff."

Saying it out loud solidified that fact as she took in Kyle's still closely shorn hair that the military had shaped. He'd traveled to the other side of the world in defense of his country, seeing and doing things she could only imagine. What could be more dashing and romantic than *that*?

"I'm sorry I don't do more of that," he said gruffly. "You deserve a guy who can tell you those things. I can try to be better, but I'm—"

"No," she broke in, even as her voice shattered. She wasn't trying to make him into someone different. He was perfect the way he was, and she'd finally opened her eyes to it. "You do something wonderful like bring me flowers, and I don't even take them. I'm just as much to blame for our problems as you are. Probably more. You'd never have left if I had just told you every day what you meant to me."

Kyle was never going to be like her dad, who left notes all over the house for her mother to find and surprised her with diamond earrings to mark the anniversary of their first date. She doubted Kyle even *knew* the anniversary of their first date.

The way Grace felt right now, none of that stuff mattered. She had a man who demonstrated his love for her in a hundred subtle ways if she'd just pay attention.

He tipped her chin up with a gentle forefinger and lightly laid his lips on hers. When he finally pulled back, he said, "But I'm not sorry I left. I gained so much from that. Foremost, the ability to come back to Royal and be a father. I was lost and being a SEAL is how I found myself. I might never have had the courage to enlist if things hadn't shaken out like they did. I'd never have had Maggie and Maddie. There was a higher power at work, and I, for one, am very grateful."

She nodded because her heart was spilling over into her throat, and she wasn't sure her voice would actually work.

Her "standards" had been a shield she'd thrown up to keep other men away, when all along her heart had belonged to this man. And then she'd kept right on using her standards as an excuse to avoid facing her own failures.

There was so much more to say, so she forced herself to open her mouth and spill all her angst about the possibility of Kyle leaving again, which had also been an excuse. It was clear he was here for good—what more proof did she need? But that didn't magically make her fears go away, much as being in love didn't magically make everything work out okay.

He let her talk, holding her hand the whole time, and then he talked. They both talked until Clare came back into the room to check on Maddie, then they talked until Maddie woke up howling for a bottle. When she fell back into an exhausted sleep, they talked some more.

When dawn peeked through the window, they hadn't slept and hadn't stopped talking. Grace had learned more about the man she loved in those few hours than in the entire span of their relationship. Even though Kyle hadn't said *I love you* again—which honestly, she could never hear often enough—and in spite of the fact that he would never be a chatterbox about his feelings, it was hands down the most romantic night of Grace's life.

If only Maddie had miraculously gotten better, it would have been a perfect start to their second chance.

When Clare Connelly came into Maddie's room shortly after dawn, Kyle had to stand up and stretch his leg. With an apologetic glance at Grace, he stood and paced around the hospital crib where his daughter lay.

He didn't want to lose that precious contact with Grace, but she didn't seem to be in a hurry to go anywhere. That could change at a moment's notice. He wished he could express how much it meant to him that she'd stayed last night. His inability to share such feelings was one of the many things that had kept them apart.

"Dr. Reese will be in shortly," Clare told them. "Why

don't you go get some breakfast while I change Maddie. You need to get some air."

Kyle nodded and grabbed Grace's hand to drag her with him, because he wasn't letting her out of his sight. Last night had been a turning point. They were in a good place. Almost. Grace deserved a guy who could spout poetry and be all the things she wanted. But she was stuck with him. If she wanted him. Nothing had been decided, and along with the concern about Maddie, everything weighed on him. He was exhausted and emotional and needed *something* in his life to be settled.

They grabbed a bite to eat and about a gallon of coffee. When they returned to Maddie's hospital room, Liam and Hadley were waiting for them. Perfect.

"Any news?" Hadley asked anxiously. "I hardly slept. I was sure we'd get a text at any moment and have to rush back to the hospital."

"Nothing yet. The doctor will be here soon. I guess we'll know more then," Kyle said.

As if Kyle had summoned him, Dr. Reese strode down the hall and nodded briefly. "I'm going to start some more tests. I'll be out to give you the results in a bit."

The four of them watched him disappear into Maddie's room. What was Kyle supposed to do now? Wait some more to find out what was happening with his daughter?

Liam cleared his throat. "Hadley and I talked, by the way. We ripped up all the adoption paperwork. We're formally withdrawing our bid for custody of your daughters. It's pretty obvious you're the best father they could hope for, and we want you to know we're here for you."

Somehow he managed to blurt out, "That's great."

Grace nodded, slipping her hand into his. "He's an amazing man and an amazing father. I wouldn't have recommended that he retain custody otherwise."

Their overwhelming support nearly did him in. He'd

left Royal to find a new team, a place where he could fit in and finally feel like a part of something, only to learn that there really was no place like home.

"Just like that?" he finally asked Liam and Hadley. "You were going to adopt Maddie and Maggie. It can't be easy to live in the same house and realize what you've missed out on."

He wouldn't take to that arrangement too well, that was for sure. If they'd somehow gotten custody, there was no way he'd have stayed. And he'd have ruined his second chance with Grace in the process. Leaving was still his go-to method for coping. But if things went the way he hoped, he had a reason to stay. Forever.

Hadley shook her head. "It's not easy. It was one of the hardest conversations we've had as a couple, but it was the easiest decision. We both love them, so much, and want the absolute best for them. Which means *you*. They're your daughters. We're incredibly fortunate for the time we've had together, and besides, you're not going anywhere, right?"

"No." Kyle tightened his grip on Grace's hand. "I'm not. Royal is where I belong."

The words spilled from his heart easily, despite never dreaming such a thing would be true.

"Then it will be fine," Liam said. "We're still their aunt and uncle, and we expect to babysit a lot in the future."

"That's a deal." Kyle shook his brother's hand and held it for a beat longer, just to solidify the brotherly bond that they were forging.

Hadley and Liam waited with Kyle and Grace, chatting about the ranch and telling stories about Hadley's cat, Waldo. Finally, the doctor emerged, and Kyle tried to read the man's face, but it was impossible to tell his daughter's prognosis from that alone.

Quickly, he stood.

"She's going to make a full recovery," Dr. Reese proclaimed. "The tests were all negative. The fever didn't cause any more damage to her heart."

Everyone started talking at once, expressing relief and giving the doctor their thanks. Numbly, Kyle shook the doctor's hand and stumbled toward Maddie's room, determined to see her for himself to confirm that she was indeed fine.

After a few minutes, Grace forced him to go home with her so he could get some sleep, but he couldn't sleep. Now that he could stop worrying about Maddie so much, he couldn't get Grace's comments about being swept off her feet out of his mind.

They'd talked, and things were looking up, but no one had made any promises. Of course, it hadn't been the time or place. They'd been in a hospital room while his daughter fought for her life.

But he owed Grace so much. And now he had to step up. This was his opportunity to give her everything her heart desired.

When Hadley called Grace to invite her to a horse show Friday night, Grace actually pulled the phone away from her ear to check and make sure it was really Hadley's name on the screen.

"I'm sorry. Did you say a horse show?" Grace repeated. "There's no horse show scheduled this time of year. Everyone is busy with calving season."

In a town like Royal, everyone lived and died by the ranch schedule whether they worked on one or not. And Kyle had been conspicuously absent for the better part of a week as he pulled calves, worked with the vet and fell into bed exhausted each night.

He always texted her a good-night message, though, no matter how late it was. She might have saved them all, even though not one had mentioned talking about the future. It had been almost a week since the hospital, and she and Kyle had had precious few moments alone together since then.

That's what happened when you fell in love with a rancher.

She'd hoped he might be the one calling her for a last-minute Friday night date so they could talk. It wasn't looking too promising since it was already six o'clock.

"Don't be difficult," Hadley scolded. "Liam is busy helping Kyle and I need some me time. Girls' night out. Come on."

Laughing, Grace said yes. Only Hadley would consider a horse show a girls' night out activity. "Your middle name should be Horse Crazy."

"It is," Hadley insisted pertly. "Says so on my birth certificate. I already asked Candace to watch the girls, so I'll pick you up in thirty minutes. Wear something nice."

Hadley was still acting in her capacity as the nanny, though often, Grace dropped by to spend time with the babies. She and Hadley had grown close as a result. Close enough that Grace felt totally comfortable calling Hadley out when she said something ridiculous.

"To a horse show?"

"Yes, ma'am. I will be dragging you out for a drink afterward, if you must know. Be there soon."

Grace chuckled as she hung up. As instructed, she donned a pink knee-length dress that hugged her curves and made her look like a knockout, if she did say so herself. Of course, she wasn't in the market to pick up an admirer, but it didn't hurt to let the male population of Royal eat their hearts out, did it?

The only arena in Royal large enough for a horse show was on the west end of downtown, and Grace was a bit surprised to see a full parking lot, given the timing.

"How come I haven't heard anything about this horse show before now?" Grace asked, her suspicions rising a notch as even more trucks poured into the lot behind them. This arena was normally the venue of choice for the county rodeo that took place during late May, and it held a good number of people.

"Because it was last-minute," Hadley said vaguely with an airy wave. "Liam has some horses in the show, and that's how I found out about it."

"Oh." There wasn't much else to do at that point but follow Hadley into the arena to a seat near the front row. "These are great seats."

"Helps to have a husband on the inside," Hadley acknowledged with a wink.

The grandstand was already half-full. Grace waved at the continual stream of people she knew, and hugged a few, like Violet McCallum, who was looking a lot better since the last time they'd seen each other. Raina Patterson and Nolan Dane strolled by, Raina's little boy in tow, as always, followed by Cade Baxter and his wife, Mellie. The foursome stopped to chat for a minute, then found seats not far away.

The lights dimmed and the show started. Sheriff Battle played the part of announcer, hamming it up with a deep voice that was so far removed from his normal tenor that Grace had to laugh. And then with a drumroll, horses galloped into the arena, crisscrossing past each other in a dizzying weave. It was a wonder they didn't hit each other, which was a testament to the stellar handling skills of the riders.

Spotlights danced over the horses as they began to fall into a formation. One by one, the horses galloped to a spot in line, nose to tail, displaying signs affixed to their sides with three-foot high letters painted on them. *G-R-A-C—*

Grace blinked. The horses were spelling her name. They

couldn't be. And then the *E* skidded into place. The line kept going. *W-I-L-L*.

Something fluttered in her heart as she started to get an inkling of what the rest of the message might possibly spell out. No. It couldn't be. "Hadley, what is all of this?"

"A surprise," Hadley announced unnecessarily, glee coating her voice. "Good thing you took my advice and wore a pretty dress."

Y-O-U. The last horse snorted as he pranced into place. And then came the next one. *M—*

Holy cow. That definitely was the right letter to start the word she fervently hoped the horses were about to spell. All at once, a commotion to her right distracted her from the horses. The spotlight slid into the stands and high-lighted a lone man making his way toward her. A man who was supposed to be in a barn at Wade Ranch. But wasn't, because he was here.

The last horse hit his mark and the sign was complete. *Grace, will you marry me?* It was the most beautiful thing in the whole world, except for the man she loved.

Her breath caught as Kyle arrived at her seat, wearing a devastating dark suit that he looked almost as delicious in as when he was wearing nothing.

She didn't dare look away as he knelt beside her and took her hand. "Hey, Grace."

Tears spilled from her suddenly full eyes, though why Kyle's standard greeting did it when nothing else thus far had was a mystery to her. "Hey, Kyle. Fancy meeting you here."

"Heard there was a horse show. It so happens I own a couple of horses. So here I am." He held up a small square box with a hinged lid. "Okay, I admit I set all this up be-cause I wanted to do this right. I love you, Grace. So much. I want nothing more than to put this ring on your finger right now, in front of all these good people."

Yes, yes, yes. A thousand times yes. There was never a possibility of anything other than becoming Mrs. Kyle Wade. She'd never expected a romantic proposal. She'd have been happy with a quiet evening at home, but this… this took the cake. It was a story for the ages, one she'd recount to Maddie and Maggie until they were sick of hearing it. Because she was going to get to be their mother.

"I'd be okay with that," she said through the lump in her throat.

"Not yet." To her grave disappointment, he snapped the box closed and pocketed it. "You asked to be swept off your feet."

And then he did exactly that. As he stood, he gathered her up in his arms and lifted her from her seat, holding her against his chest as if he meant to never let go.

She'd be okay with that, too.

The crowd cheered. She noted Hadley clapping out of the corner of her eye as Kyle began climbing the stairs toward the exit, carrying Grace in his strong arms.

Kyle spoke into her ear. "I hope you won't be disappointed, but you're missing the rest of the show."

She shook her head, clinging to Kyle's amazingly solid shoulders. "I'm not missing anything. This is the best show in town, right here."

Looked as if she was an excellent judge of character after all.

Once he had her outside, he set her down and pulled her into his embrace for a kiss that was both tender and fierce all at the same time.

When he let go, she saw that a long black stretch limousine had rolled to a stop near them. "What is this?"

"Part of sweeping you off your feet," Kyle acknowledged. "Now that Maddie has fully recovered, I'm whisking you away on a romantic weekend, just you and me, to celebrate our engagement. But I want to make it official."

Then he pulled the box from his pocket and slid the huge emerald-cut diamond ring onto her finger. It winked in the moonlight and was the most beautiful thing she'd ever seen. Except for the man she loved. "Tell me this is forever, Kyle."

He nodded. "Forever. I'm not going anywhere. I'm a part of something valuable. I'm a cattle rancher now with orders pouring in for the calves I've helped deliver. The Texas Cattlemen's Club voted me in as a member earlier today. My daughters are thriving, and I'm going to get the best woman in the world as a wife. Why would I want to leave?"

"Good answer," she said as the tears flowed again. "But if you did decide you wanted to leave for whatever reason, I'd follow you."

"You would?" This seemed like news to him for some odd reason.

"Of course. I love you. I know now I could never be happy without you, so..." She shrugged. "Where you go, I go. We're a team now. Team Wade, four strong. And maybe more after we get the first round out of diapers."

He laughed softly. "I like the sound of that. Keep talking."

* * * * *

Don't miss a single installment of
TEXAS CATTLEMEN'S CLUB; LIES AND LULLABIES

BABY SECRETS AND A SCHEMING SHEIKH
ROCK ROYAL, TEXAS

COURTING THE COWBOY BOSS
by USA TODAY *bestselling author Janice Maynard*

LONE STAR HOLIDAY PROPOSAL
by USA TODAY *bestselling author Yvonne Lindsay*

NANNY MAKES THREE
by Cat Schield

THE DOCTOR'S BABY DARE
by USA TODAY *bestselling author Michelle Celmer*

THE SEAL'S SECRET HEIRS
by Kat Cantrell

A SURPRISE FOR THE SHEIKH
by Sarah M. Anderson

IN PURSUIT OF HIS WIFE
by Kristi Gold

A BRIDE FOR THE BOSS
by USA TODAY *bestselling author Maureen Child*

If you're on Twitter, tell us what you think of
Harlequin Desire! #harlequindesire

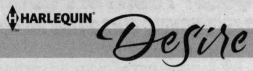
#2437 TAKE ME, COWBOY
Copper Ridge • by Maisey Yates
Tomboy Anna Brown *wants* to tap into her femininity, but is clueless on *how* to do so. When her brothers bet she'll be dateless at a charity auction, she turns to a makeover—and her way-too-sexy best friend—to prove them wrong.

#2438 HIS BABY AGENDA
Billionaires and Babies • by Katherine Garbera
Gabi De La Cruz thought she'd found Mr. Right...until he was arrested for murder! Now he's back and needs help with his young child, but is there room for a second chance when he's obsessed with clearing his name?

#2439 A SURPRISE FOR THE SHEIKH
Texas Cattleman's Club: Lies and Lullabies
by Sarah M. Anderson
Sheikh Rafe bin Saleed wants revenge, and he'll buy Royal, Texas, to get it. But will a night of unplanned passion with his enemy's sister give him a baby he didn't bargain for?

#2440 A BARGAIN WITH THE BOSS
Chicago Sons • by Barbara Dunlop
Playboy brother Tucker has no desire to run the family corporation, but a scandal forces his hand. His trial by fire heats up even more when he clashes with the feisty, sexy secretary who's hiding a big secret from him...

#2441 REUNITED WITH THE REBEL BILLIONAIRE
Bayou Billionaires • by Catherine Mann
After being ordered to reunite with his estranged wife to keep his career stable, a football superstar realizes that their fake relationship is more than an assignment. It might be what he wants more than anything else...

#2442 SECRET CHILD, ROYAL SCANDAL
The Sherdana Royals • by Cat Schield
Marrying his former lover to legitimize his secret son's claim to the throne becomes more challenging than prince Christian Alessandro expected. Because Noelle Dubonne makes a demand of her own—it's true love or nothing!

REQUEST YOUR FREE BOOKS!
2 FREE NOVELS PLUS 2 FREE GIFTS!

H HARLEQUIN®

Desire

ALWAYS POWERFUL, PASSIONATE AND PROVOCATIVE

YES! Please send me 2 FREE Harlequin® Desire novels and my 2 FREE gifts (gifts are worth about $10). After receiving them, if I don't wish to receive any more books, I can return the shipping statement marked "cancel." If I don't cancel, I will receive 6 brand-new novels every month and be billed just $4.55 per book in the U.S. or $5.24 per book in Canada. That's a savings of at least 13% off the cover price! It's quite a bargain! Shipping and handling is just 50¢ per book in the U.S. and 75¢ per book in Canada.* I understand that accepting the 2 free books and gifts places me under no obligation to buy anything. I can always return a shipment and cancel at any time. Even if I never buy another book, the two free books and gifts are mine to keep forever.

225/326 HDN GH2P

Name	(PLEASE PRINT)	
Address		Apt. #
City	State/Prov.	Zip/Postal Code

Signature (if under 18, a parent or guardian must sign)

Mail to the **Reader Service:**
IN U.S.A.: P.O. Box 1867, Buffalo, NY 14240-1867
IN CANADA: P.O. Box 609, Fort Erie, Ontario L2A 5X3

Want to try two free books from another line?
Call 1-800-873-8635 or visit www.ReaderService.com.

* Terms and prices subject to change without notice. Prices do not include applicable taxes. Sales tax applicable in N.Y. Canadian residents will be charged applicable taxes. Offer not valid in Quebec. This offer is limited to one order per household. Not valid for current subscribers to Harlequin Desire books. All orders subject to credit approval. Credit or debit balances in a customer's account(s) may be offset by any other outstanding balance owed by or to the customer. Please allow 4 to 6 weeks for delivery. Offer available while quantities last.

Your Privacy—The Reader Service is committed to protecting your privacy. Our Privacy Policy is available online at www.ReaderService.com or upon request from the Reader Service.

We make a portion of our mailing list available to reputable third parties that offer products we believe may interest you. If you prefer that we not exchange your name with third parties, or if you wish to clarify or modify your communication preferences, please visit us at www.ReaderService.com/consumerchoice or write to us at Reader Service Preference Service, P.O. Box 9062, Buffalo, NY 14240-9062. Include your complete name and address.

Anna dropped the towel and unzipped the bag, staring at
the contents with no small amount of horror. There was…
underwear inside it. Underwear that Chase had purchased
for her for their first fake date. She grabbed the pair of
panties that were attached to a little hanger. Oh, they had
no back. She supposed guessing her size didn't matter
much. She swallowed hard, rubbing her thumb over
the soft material. He would know exactly what she was
wearing beneath the dress. Would know just how little
that was.

*He isn't going to think about it. Because he doesn't
think about you that way.*

He never had. He never would. She was never going
to touch him, either. She'd made that decision a long time
ago. For a lot of reasons that were as valid today as they
had been the very first time he'd ever made her stomach
jump when she looked at him.

She tugged on the clothes, having to do a pretty intense
wiggle to get the slinky red dress up all the way before

zipping it into place. She took a deep breath, turned around. She faced her reflection in the mirror full-on. She looked… Well, her hair was wet and straggly, and she looked half-drowned. She didn't look curvy, or shimmery, or delightful. She sighed heavily, trying to ignore the sinking feeling in her stomach.

Chase really was going to have to be a miracle worker in order to pull this off.

"Buck up," she said to herself.

So what was one more moment of feeling inadequate? Honestly, in the broad tapestry of her life it would barely register. She was never quite what was expected. She never quite fit. So why'd she expect that she was going to put on a sexy dress and suddenly be transformed into the kind of sex kitten she didn't even want to be?

She gritted her teeth, throwing open the bedroom door and walking into the room. "I hope you're happy," she said, flinging her arms wide. "You get what you get."

Chase, who had been completely silent upon her entry into the room, remained so. She glared at him. He wasn't saying anything. He was only staring. "Well?"

"It's nice," he said.

His voice sounded rough, and kind of thin.

"You're a liar."

"I'm not a liar."

"Are you satisfied?" she asked.

His jaw tensed, a muscle in his cheek ticking. "I guess you could say that."

Don't miss TAKE ME, COWBOY by USA TODAY bestselling author Maisey Yates available April 2016 wherever Harlequin® Desire books and ebooks are sold.

Whatever You're Into... Passionate Reads

Looking for more passionate reads from Harlequin®?
Fear not! Harlequin® Presents, Harlequin® Desire and
Harlequin® Blaze offer you irresistible romance stories
featuring powerful heroes.

◆HARLEQUIN *Presents.*

Do you want alpha males, decadent glamour and jet-set
lifestyles? Step into the sensational, sophisticated world of
Harlequin® Presents, where sinfully tempting heroes ignite a
fierce and wickedly irresistible passion!

◆HARLEQUIN *Desire*

Harlequin® Desire novels are powerful, passionate and
provocative contemporary romances set against a backdrop of
wealth, privilege and sweeping family saga. Alpha heroes with
a soft side meet strong-willed but vulnerable heroines amid a
dramatic world of divided loyalties, high-stakes conflict and
intense emotion.

◆HARLEQUIN *Blaze*

Harlequin® Blaze stories sizzle with strong heroines and
irresistible heroes playing the game of modern love and lust.
They're fun, sexy and always steamy.

Be sure to check out our full selection of books
within each series every month!

www.Harlequin.com